P9-DIA-116

THE ABSENCE OF SPARROWS

THE ABSENCE OF SPARROWS

BY KURT KIRCHMEIER

Little, Brown and Company
New York Boston

Little, Brown and Company
Hachette Book Group
1290 Avenue of the Americas, New York, NY 10104
Visit us at LBYR.com

First Edition: May 2019

Little, Brown and Company is a division of Hachette Book Group, Inc. The Little, Brown name and logo are trademarks of Hachette Book Group, Inc.

The publisher is not responsible for websites (or their content) that are not owned by the publisher.

Library of Congress Cataloging-in-Publication Data
Names: Kirchmeier, Kurt, author.
Title: The absence of sparrows: a novel / by Kurt Kirchmeier.
Description: First edition. | New York; Boston: Little, Brown and Company, 2019. | Summary: Eleven-year-old bird watcher Ben must defy his brother to save their father after the glass plague sweeps through their town and a voice on the radio demands the simultaneous shattering of all plague victims.
Identifiers: LCCN 2018020155| ISBN 9780316450928 (hardcover) | ISBN 9780316450911 (ebook) | ISBN 9780316528825 (library edition ebook)
Subjects: | CYAC: Family life—Fiction. | Brothers—Fiction. | Epidemics—Fiction. | Birds—Fiction.
Classification: LCC PZ7.1.K623 Abs 2019 | DDC [Fic]—dc23
LC record available at https://lccn.loc.gov/2018020155

ISBNs: 978-0-316-45092-8 (hardcover), 978-0-316-45091-1 (ebook)

Printed in the United States of America

LSC-C

10 9 8 7 6 5 4 3 2 1

For Anna, for everything

When I look back on that summer, I think about birds. I think about crows and sparrows and waxwings, hawks and shrikes and jays. I guess you could say it's just a distraction, a way for me to keep the truth of what actually happened to the back of my mind, but there's more to it than that. It was through birds that I learned to see the world more clearly, both during the plague, and after.

I used to wonder how something so small and delicate as a ruby-throated hummingbird could possibly fly nonstop across the entire Gulf of Mexico, a journey of five hundred miles and more than five million wingbeats, over nothing but cold, open water, but I think I understand now. They do it because they have to, because that's the path that fate chose for them, however unfairly. Ruby-throated hummingbirds are survivors, and so are we. That summer was our Gulf of Mexico, and somehow we crossed it. But not all of us, and not unscathed.

It all started on a blistering hot day in early July....

ONE

C'mon," said Pete. "Stop being a doofus."

I was avoiding the cracks on the sidewalk again, like we both used to do when we were younger and we'd race to the end of the block while trying our best not to break Mom's back along the way. Pete always won, but I'm pretty sure Mom got crippled every time.

"It's harder than it used to be," I said. "There's way more cracks." Plus, my feet had grown a few shoe sizes.

I finally gave up, my attention turning to the sound of a black-capped chickadee singing from somewhere nearby. Black-capped chickadees were one of my favorite birds. Pete didn't have favorite birds, and seemed to think that I shouldn't either. It wasn't *normal.*

I could hear a northern flicker in the distance as well, with its long and loud *wick-wick-wick* sound. Flickers are big woodpeckers with exotic-looking markings. The first time I saw one, I thought I was looking at something that didn't belong, a rare specimen that must have gotten lost during its migration. Turns out they're actually common, but you don't see them much because they're skittish around people. Unlike chickadees.

Pete continued on without me. I listened a moment longer and then ran to catch up.

We were on our way to our uncle Dean's shop, or more precisely, the shop roof, which was one of our two favorite haunts. The other was up in the arms of the big silver maple in Sunskill Park, the one with the checkered kite stuck fast near the top. Pete was hell-bent on someday freeing the kite, but could never quite work up the courage to risk putting his weight on those bendy little branches. Not even if I double-dog dared him.

As was always the case when we knew we'd be up on the roof, we both stopped along the way to stuff our pockets with maple seedpods, or propeller leaves, as we called them, since that's what they looked like when you dropped them: spinning propellers. I thought it amazing how nature sometimes made the best toys. Not that we ever called them toys, of course. Toys were for kids. Pete was twelve and I was eleven, and dropping maple seedpods from the roof of Uncle Dean's shop was serious business. There was a root beer on the line.

"Storm's coming," said Pete when we arrived at our destination. He kept his eyes skyward as he climbed the ladder attached to the wall at the back of the shop.

Pete had been acting like some kind of weather expert ever since predicting a tornado last summer. It ripped through Stanley Peterson's farm, dancing between a few grain silos before finally picking up and dropping Stanley's riding lawn mower onto the roof of his burgundy Cadillac. That was the only damage, which is kind of weird when you think about it, especially since people used to say Stanley spent more time with that car than he did with his wife. He used to polish it at least once a day. Pastor Nolan told Dad that it was God's way of punishing Stanley for his vanity. I don't know if that's true, but what I do know is that Stanley started driving a little old rust bucket shortly thereafter. I guess he didn't want to press his luck.

Pete's prediction that day wasn't anything special. He'd been making the same one regularly for almost two months. He would quirk an eye at the sky and say, "It's going to storm." If it didn't, it was no big deal, and he'd just act like he never said anything in the first place. But if it did happen to storm, he'd look at you all sage-like and say, "See? I told you."

"Maybe," I said as I stepped off the ladder and onto the roof, although the clouds didn't really look stormy to me at all. They had a soft-edged fuzziness about them, not that crisp popcorn shape of growing thunderheads.

We made our way to the front of the roof, where the garage overlooks Main Street. Uncle Dean was one of only two mechanics in Griever's Mill (population 3,004), but even so, the shop was never all that busy. Nobody took any notice of us as we parked our butts and let our legs dangle over the edge. On the sidewalk directly below us was a white chalk circle with a big X through it. This was our target, the landing pad for our seedpods. The first one to hit it would earn himself bragging rights for a whole week, plus the loser would owe him a root beer float.

"You go first," Pete told me, as usual.

"I always go first," I argued. The wind invariably took the first pod. If I went first, Pete could try to compensate for which way it was blowing.

"I went first last time," he lied. Or maybe he was just misremembering. That wasn't uncommon with Pete.

"Fine," I said. What Pete didn't realize was that I'd come prepared this time, and had a single blade of grass to go along with my propeller leaves. I took it out of my pocket and tossed it into the wind.

"Hey, that's cheating, Ben!" said Pete.

"So is making me go first all the time," I countered.

We both watched as the blade of grass landed well left of the target.

"Be a cheater, then," said Pete. "See if I care. You'll still miss."

I probably would. The best either of us had ever done was getting it on our fifth try.

"Definitely going to storm," Pete said as I lined up for my drop. "Clouds are already turning black out past the edge of town."

"Shh," I said. "I'm trying to concentrate."

Pete scoffed. "I bet you don't even land within ten feet of it."

"Not this time," I said with a sudden certainty that sprang from I don't know where. Somehow I just knew that I wasn't going to miss, that I was going to nail it the first try, like when an athlete gets into the zone and knows he's going to score a goal or get a touchdown.

My propeller spun as if guided by fate, around and around in slow motion, the wind pulling it away and then pushing it back into line again. Its ten-second journey from rooftop to sidewalk felt to me more like ten minutes, but it finally landed gently at the very center of the X. I let out a whoop while Pete called me a cheater, but my gloating pretty much ended there.

When I looked up from the makeshift landing pad, my eyes were immediately drawn to the darkening sky that Pete had mentioned just moments before.

"Uh, Pete," I said. "I don't think those are clouds. . . ."

TWO

They definitely weren't clouds.

Dust storm? I wondered, but even as the thought took form, I knew it was wrong. What I was seeing looked more like coal smoke, the kind you'd see billowing out from a locomotive, all thick and dark woolen gray. It didn't disperse like smoke, though; it held together as if buffeted by winds from every side, a roiling mass as wide as our town, yet strangely flat, almost pancake shaped. It was getting closer, its underside maybe thirty feet off the ground and its leading edge about two football fields away. It drifted with all the silence of morning fog, and yet something about it seemed predatory, like a lion on the savanna stalking a kill.

An icy chill climbed the length of my spine—a sensation immediately followed by a sudden and urgent desire to get down off the roof.

"C'mon," I told Pete, but he just stood there and kept on staring.

"Pete!" I yelled.

He finally snapped out of it and looked at me.

"We need to go," I told him.

"Yeah," he agreed. "Definitely."

By the time we'd climbed down and circled around to the front of the garage, the darkness had already reached the far end of the street. Others had noticed it, too, and a small crowd stood on the sidewalk in front of the shops to watch it approach. I rescued my maple seedpod from the landing pad before anyone could step on it. I thought it might be lucky, and I wanted to keep it for next time.

Uncle Dean saw us from inside and came out to join us, not noticing what else was going on.

"What're you boys up to?" he said, adjusting his ball cap. Uncle Dean was always adjusting his ball cap. It was like he couldn't quite make it comfortable on his head, even though he'd been wearing it for as long as I could remember.

"Just watching," said Pete.

Uncle Dean followed our gazes out to the approaching dark. His lips parted as his jaw went slack. "What in the name of H. P. Lovecraft is that?"

I had no idea who H. P. Lovecraft was, so I just shook my head and replied, "Not clouds." I knew that wasn't helpful at all.

Across the street was Crandall's General Store. Mr. Crandall was standing on the sidewalk by the front door, hollering in at his wife, Marge. "Hurry up and get out here!" he said. "You gotta see this!"

"Whatever it is," Uncle Dean continued, "I don't like the looks of it. C'mon, let's get you boys inside."

I was already three steps ahead of him, my thinking being that whatever was happening, it would probably be a whole lot safer beneath a roof and surrounded by walls. Once inside, I waited for something like a sudden gust of wind or a downpour of smoky-colored raindrops, but even as the darkness slid over the sky right above us, the only thing that seemed to change was that the neighborhood sparrows—regular house sparrows, mostly—immediately stopped their chirping and flying and took up silent perches on eaves and fences, their small bills turned up at the heavens, heads cocked as though they were listening.

I wondered if they sensed something that we humans couldn't. I watched them for a moment through the grimy glass of a single-pane window. Pete stayed close beside me, his eyes never leaving the sky.

"I had a dream like this once," he whispered, "except I was lost in a cornfield."

Outside it wasn't night dark, but more like solar-eclipse dark, or at least what I imagined that to be. What little light there was had a different quality to it, a sort of peculiarity that made me think of all the "totality" YouTube videos that my science teacher made us watch in class last year, when half the country seemed to be suffering from total-eclipse fever.

Uncle Dean headed off to the corner to call Dad on his CB radio, since he was most likely still out driving around in the country, where cell phone coverage was spotty. Dad was an assessor for an insurance company, which meant that he did stuff like write up estimates for hail-damaged crops. He was also a volunteer fireman, and a first responder, too. I listened as the static gave way to conversation. I couldn't make out what Dad was saying from across the garage—the transmission was too crackly—but I could hear Uncle Dean.

"Logan? Hey, whereabouts are you?" He paused, listening and nodding. "Yeah, it's right above us here in town. Bloody bizarre. I've got your two birds here under my wing. Caught 'em flying down from my roof again." Another pause. More static. "I will. Don't you worry. Let me know if you hear anything, all right? Yep, you too, stay safe." He hung up the CB and rejoined us at the window.

"What'd he say?" asked Pete.

"He says the sky's clear where he is, but he can see the dark in the distance. He's on his way back now and wants you two to stay put."

"What about Mom?" I asked.

"I told your dad I'd call her on the phone. I'm sure she's safe at home, though. Nothing to worry about."

I wasn't so sure. Mom could get a little anxious sometimes. Like when I was eight and someone reported a cougar near the edge of town. Pete and I weren't allowed in the backyard for almost a week. I could just imagine what was going to happen because of this. She'd probably have us both on leashes.

I went back to staring out the window. The darkness hovered above the whole town now and everyone had gone back inside except for old man Crandall, who was still out on the sidewalk, brandishing one of those Polaroid cameras that would spit out a picture right after you took it. You couldn't look at the photo right away, though; you had to wait for the developing chemicals to dry first.

I watched as Mr. Crandall snapped a picture and then tried to speed the drying process by waving the photo back and forth in the air. Mrs. Crandall yelled at him from the doorway, her eyes moving between her husband and the dark above, as if a coal-black funnel might suddenly appear to swallow him up.

"For heaven's sake, George!" she said. She finally stepped over the threshold and reached out, clearly intent on dragging him if that's what it came to.

She never got the chance, though. One second she was reaching, and the next she was standing there wide-eyed, staring down at George Crandall's right hand, which was black now, I realized, and shiny as volcanic rock.

The Polaroid camera crashed to the pavement as the old man seemed to lose all control of his fingers.

"It's spreading," I heard Pete say. And it was.

From his hand to his wrist and then right up his sleeve—by the time my brain even registered what was happening, the blackness had claimed his whole arm and part of his neck above his collar, and it didn't stop there.

Mr. Crandall opened his mouth as if to cry out, but it was already too late; the darkness had seized his vocal cords. A moment later the transformation was complete.

George Crandall stood frozen in place, an obsidian statue dressed in an old wool suit with patches on the elbows. A crow flew down to land on the statue's head. It cawed twice and then silently flew off south.

THREE

The lights inside the garage flickered twice and then went out completely. The shop radio cut out as well, but not before losing its signal for a moment first, the harsh white noise giving way to a silence broken only by the hysterical wails of poor Mrs. Crandall, who was still on her knees on the sidewalk.

Seeing her out there seemed to trigger something in Uncle Dean's brain, a hardwired instinct to help. He started toward the door, with Pete following close on his heels.

"Just wait!" I told them both. I was worried that it

wasn't safe yet, that the worst might still be to come, even though the sky was already clearing, the smoky darkness moving off with all the stealth and mystery of a town-sized UFO.

They both ignored me and continued out onto the street, where several others were already gathering, their eyes wary and their movements slow, like they'd just crawled out from a bunker in the midst of a war, the prospect of further bombing hanging over their heads.

I only made it as far as the front door myself before deciding to wait inside, at least for a moment or two, just in case. I tried to tell myself that I was the smart one, that I was only being sensible, but when it came right down to it, I was just scared.

I watched as Pete and Uncle Dean broke away from each other, with Pete heading off for a closer look at the old-man-turned-statue while Uncle Dean went to help Mrs. Crandall back to her feet. Uncle Dean was quickly joined by the large-bottomed Spandex sisters, who owned the hair salon down the street. Their last name wasn't actually Spandex, but that's what we called them since that's what they always wore. Pete usually made a rude joke whenever he saw them, but today his head didn't even turn in their direction. He was mesmerized.

"It's not possible," someone in the growing crowd said. "It can't be."

Clearly it was, though. The longtime owner of the general store had turned to glass.

I jumped as the radio behind me crackled back to life. The lights came back on as well, which made me feel a little bit better. Whatever had happened was officially done happening... for the time being at any rate.

I screwed up my courage and joined all the other brave people out on the street, most of whom had formed a circle around Mr. Crandall. I pushed my way into the heart of it to try to find Pete, who of course had moved in closer than everyone else, a slave to his curiosity.

"Nobody touch him!" said a woman to my right, as if Mr. Crandall's condition might be contagious, which, for all we knew, it was.

Everyone backed off a step. Everyone except Pete. Ignoring both the warning and plain common sense, he stepped right up and reached out his hand to tap

Mr. Crandall square on the chin. It made a firm sound, like a fingernail against granite.

"My God," said a bearded man in a John Deere baseball cap. "What if he's still in there? Trapped? He'll suffocate to death!"

"I don't think it's like a shell," Pete said. Mr. Crandall's mouth was still open, and you could clearly tell that it was black on the inside, too. I wasn't tall enough to see if the darkness went all the way down, but the bearded man was. He stepped forward for a closer look.

"I think he's solid through and through," he told the crowd.

The whole street was buzzing. The few people who had actually witnessed the transformation were now trying to explain what had happened to those who had shown up too late to see it. Many of them were talking over each other, which only resulted in shouting.

I was standing close enough now to see that every small detail was retained in the glass, from the lines on Mr. Crandall's knuckles to the hair in his ears, which I'd noticed one day in church a few months before and hadn't been able to *stop* noticing ever since, mostly because it grossed me out a little. Mr. Crandall wasn't just a frozen semblance of his former self—he was a flawless replica, as dark as onyx but scarily real.

I couldn't bring myself to look at his eyes, and instead turned my gaze to the Polaroid photo, which I'd belatedly noticed he was still holding above his head. It seemed important up there, like a small flag or a sign of protest. I decided that I wanted to see it. I didn't know why, exactly; I just wanted to.

A small jump and the photo was mine. I only had time for a quick look before Uncle Dean appeared to pull me out of the crowd, but I was surprised to see that it hadn't finished developing yet. There was still a big dark blur right in the middle.

"C'mon," Uncle Dean said as I slipped the photo into my back pocket. "Let's get you boys back inside before your dad shows up." With one hand on my shoulder and the other on Pete's, he guided us toward his garage.

FOUR

According to Uncle Dean's shop radio, the skies were going dark all over. From New York to New Mexico, Cairo to Japan, black waves were sweeping the globe, leaving swaths of solid glass victims in their wake. Mr. Crandall wasn't alone.

If I hadn't already seen it with my own eyes, I probably wouldn't have believed what I was hearing. I would have written it off as some sort of silly mistake or misunderstanding, like when people started spreading fake news after Orson Welles read that *War of the Worlds* book over the radio. But as impossible as it seemed, it was happening. Pete and I really had just finished watching five strong men struggle to tip Mr. Crandall onto a trolley and cart him inside his general store.

It was a scene too strange for words.

"Must be heavy" was Pete's only comment on the effort, as if the men were moving a deep freeze instead of a person.

I wondered where they would put him. In the back with the stock? Maybe near the front entrance? I imagined him standing there, his hand raised as if to welcome incoming customers, like an obsidian Walmart greeter. *Definitely* too strange for words.

By the time Dad showed up, Pete and I had left the window for a pair of rickety old stools by the Coke machine. We wanted to be closer to the radio, which continued to spill bad news. A radiographer in Chicago had turned to glass while performing an X-ray; a tailor in Montreal fell victim while taking measurements for a tuxedo. It didn't seem to matter where you were when the darkness passed; inside or out, there was nowhere to hide.

"It's a bloody circus out there," said Dad as he entered the shop. The street was still abuzz over what had happened.

Pete hopped off his stool. "Did you see him? Old man Crandall?"

Dad narrowed his eyes. "George? No, why?"

"Please tell me you've been listening to the radio," said Uncle Dean.

Dad shook his head. "Signal was mostly static outside of town, so I turned it off. What's going on?" The fact that the sky had cleared had obviously left him with the impression that everything was okay.

Pete immediately launched into a breathless account of what had happened, but it was obvious that Dad was having trouble trying to follow. "Whoa," he kept saying. "Just wait. What?"

"I think you better see for yourself," Uncle Dean finally said. "C'mon."

Pete and I tried to follow, but Uncle Dean told us to wait behind and listen for any updates.

"I bet it's aliens," Pete said after they were gone. "Abductions."

"Why would they turn to glass if they got abducted?" I asked him.

He shrugged. "Maybe the aliens can't move matter without replacing it with something else. It would just be empty space otherwise. I think I saw something like that in a comic book once."

I knew it had to have come from a comic book because Pete didn't have the imagination to dream it up on his own. My brother was pretty smart, and way better at sports than I was, but he wasn't exactly a creative thinker. Still, I couldn't really argue that it *wasn't* aliens.

I started thinking then about all the books that I'd read, too, from ones about demons and monsters to others about interdimensional beings and time-traveling bounty hunters. A thousand fantastical ideas suddenly didn't seem that fantastic.

It wasn't long before Dad and Uncle Dean returned, Dad now wearing an expression unlike any I'd ever seen on his face before—sort of a mix of shock and resolve, like part of him couldn't quite believe what he had just seen, while another part had already processed it all and moved on, its focus shifting to being a dad.

"I think that's enough news for now," he said to me and Pete as we both watched him from our stools. "It's time we got home. Your mom's probably worried sick."

"Do you think the power went out at home, too?" I asked, as if that was the one thing we should be worried about.

"Hard to say" was Dad's only reply. "C'mon now, let's go."

"Is Uncle Dean coming with us?" asked Pete.

"He'll come by later," Dad replied for his brother, as if the two of them had already talked it over, which maybe they had. "He's going to keep an eye on things around here for a little while first."

What things? I almost asked, but the answer was obvious: Mr. Crandall. Uncle Dean was going to stick around just in case something changed or, perhaps, changed *back*.

We got in the truck and left for home. As always, Pete had to sit shotgun because the backseat of the truck was "too cramped" and his legs "too long." It wasn't true, but I didn't argue about it.

"Do you think it could be aliens?" I asked Dad. I was still mulling over what Pete had said earlier.

"I sincerely doubt it, Ben," he answered.

"But you don't *know* that," said Pete. "That black cloud could've been a UFO."

"It could have been a lot of things," Dad replied.

"Like what?" Pete pressed. When it came to Dad, Pete was always pressing. Mom said they liked to push each other's buttons.

"Maybe something atmospheric," I chimed in, hoping to stop them from arguing before they got started. "Like the aurora borealis, only instead of there being light in the darkness, there's darkness in the light."

"That's stupid," Pete said.

"No it's not," I countered. "It's more scientific than just blaming aliens."

Pete scoffed. "Scientific? You just made it up!"

"All right," said Dad, "that's enough. How about we leave the speculating to the experts?"

I couldn't see from the backseat, but I'm guessing that Pete rolled his eyes. He definitely shook his head. He reached forward then to turn on the radio, but it still wasn't coming in very good, probably because the antenna was snapped off halfway up. It had been that way for a while. Pete and I suspected that the Messam twins had done it, but we had no proof.

Mom came charging out of the house before Dad even got the truck into park.

"Hurry up!" she said. "Get inside!"

I almost expected her to say, *The sky is falling! The sky is falling!*

"Easy now," said Dad, getting out. "Let's everybody just stay calm."

"Calm?" said Mom. "People are turning to glass, Logan! Glass!"

"We don't know that it's glass," said Dad, as if the exact nature of the substance mattered at all. He was just trying to be reasonable, I knew. Trying to take it all in stride. I was glad for it, too—it made me feel less worried.

The TV was already on once we got inside. Normally Mom didn't watch it much, preferring to watch the birds at the feeders out in the yard, but I guess with circumstances being what they were, she felt the birds could wait. There was a big BREAKING NEWS rectangle covering a third of the screen.

It occurred to me as we all gathered around that it was the first time in a long time that we'd watched TV as a whole family, and it was weird, too, because none of us were sitting down. We watched and listened standing up, as if we might suddenly need to run.

FIVE

The reporters kept on reporting, although it soon became clear that none of them knew anything more than the guy on the radio had back at Uncle Dean's garage. It was just the same stuff happening in different places, dark skies and strange transformations, and a growing worry that this might only be the beginning.

"I don't understand," said Mom. "How can they not know anything yet? Surely there must be something they could measure or evaluate. Something in the air."

"Tests take time," said Dad.

We'd been home for about an hour, most of which

Mom had spent on the phone, trying to get in touch with long-distance relatives (except for Uncle Dean, none of our family lived within a hundred miles). She couldn't get through, though. The lines were all overloaded.

"This is stupid," said Pete, abandoning the couch and the TV for the corner nook in the dining room where our family computer was set up. He was obviously hoping to dig some answers up online. I hadn't told him that when I tried to boot the computer up the day before, the screen had gone blue and stayed that way.

"What the heck is going on?" said Pete as he turned the monitor on and off.

"Something wrong?" I asked, deciding just to play stupid. It wasn't as if I had done anything to break it, but if I said something now, Pete would blame me.

He ignored me and tried restarting it, but it was no use; the screen remained a solid blue. He swore, and Dad replied, "Hey! Watch your language."

"It's not working!" said Pete.

"Yeah, well, cursing's not going to fix it."

"Can you look at it?" Pete asked him.

"I don't see what the point would be," said Dad. "You know more about that thing than I do."

Pete gave a frustrated sigh. "What about Uncle Dean?"

"I'll ask him later," said Dad. "Let's not worry about it just this minute."

Mom tried the phone again but still couldn't get through. She started pacing. "I feel like I should be *doing* something," she finally said. "Like canning food or digging out all our candles."

Dad shrugged. "Might not be a bad idea. The candles, at least. Can't be too prepared."

"Prepared for what?" asked Pete. "Is the power gonna go out again?"

"Hard to say," Dad replied. "But there's no harm in taking a few precautions. Speaking of which, why don't you go out to the garage and get the camping lantern. It should be on a hook near the rafters. Grab the kerosene off the shelf as well."

Pete started to grumble—Pete hardly did *anything* without grumbling—but then Mom said, "Hold on. I don't think we should be going outside. Not yet."

Our garage faced the alley and was separate from the house. The distance between them was only fifteen feet. Going from one to the other and back again was barely going outside at all.

"It'll be fine," Dad told Pete. "Go on."

Mom gave him a stern look. She hated being overruled.

"People are turning to glass inside their basements, Jane," Dad reminded her. "I don't think it matters where they are. Besides, the sky is clear and blue right now. Nothing to fear."

"I suppose," she replied with a sigh.

"What should I do?" I asked.

"Why don't you go fill the feeders?" Dad said. "I'm sure the birds would appreciate it."

I suspected it wasn't really the birds he was thinking about. More likely he just wanted to talk to Mom alone for a minute, on account of her anxiety. It could get pretty bad sometimes. Bad enough that she had to take pills for it.

I wasn't supposed to know about that—the pills, I mean—but I did. I found them in the medicine cabinet one day after falling off my bike and scraping my elbow. I was just looking for a Band-Aid and there it was, a little orange bottle full of capsules. Big capsules. When I asked Dad about them, he told me they were just antibiotics and not to worry about it, which I probably wouldn't have if he hadn't hesitated in a weird way before answering me. It was just for a second, but I noticed, so I memorized the name on the bottle (alprazolam), and the next time I was at the library I looked it up. Dad had lied to me.

At first I was mad, but as I read about anxiety I understood. He just didn't want me losing sleep over Mom was all. I never told Pete about it, partly because I didn't want him worrying either, but also because I knew he wouldn't be able to keep his mouth shut.

"I already topped up the nuts and seeds today," Mom told me. "But I guess you can refill the suet cages."

Certain birds preferred different types of food, so we always had a good variety for them to choose from. Blue jays, for instance, were particularly fond of peanuts—shelled or otherwise—while suet blocks were a favorite among downy and hairy woodpeckers.

I grabbed two packages and went outside. As always, the birds scattered at my approach, and then returned as soon as the suet cages were full and my back was to them. Birds fear eye contact. That's why some butterflies have spots that look like eyes on their wings. The birds would eat them if they didn't.

I walked over to the bench by the flower bed and

sat there. Mom always watched the birds from here, binoculars in her hands and a small notebook beside her, for jotting down "field notes." The bench was far enough away from the feeders so as not to make the birds nervous.

I watched as a dozen or so of our resident house sparrows flew back and forth from the suet to the short bush that ran alongside the fence. There were two older males with big dark bibs and a bunch of females that were almost identical, the only exception being one that had a pair of pure white wings instead of the usual brown. Mom called this her special bird, her "angel sparrow," but in truth the bird was just partially leucistic, which meant that it had a pigmentation problem. The bird's wings weren't the only thing that set it apart, though; it was also less wary than the other sparrows and would sometimes stay on a branch even after the rest of its flock flew off, its little head tilted in a way that made you wonder if the bird was curious, or maybe even interested in what we were up to.

Pete came out of the garage with not only the lantern and kerosene that Dad had asked for but also an old black radio about the size of a lunch box. I immediately recognized it from a camping trip we'd taken a few years before. Dad had brought it along. I think it was his from when he was younger. I couldn't remember having seen it since, though.

"So we can listen to the news in our room," Pete explained. If we'd had cell phones like some of our friends did, it would have been easy to follow along with what was happening, but Mom and Dad said we had to wait until we were thirteen. "You'll thank me when you get older," Dad liked to say whenever Pete brought it up, although he never actually explained *why* we would thank him. I think it had something to do with having proper childhoods.

"Good idea," I said. Pete didn't have those often, so I liked to give him credit when he did.

Inside, Pete took the radio up to our room and then came back down and joined me on the floor in front of the TV, much like he used to on Saturday mornings when we watched cartoons, many of which I still watched by myself, while Pete had now "grown out of them," as he liked to say. If that was true, then how come he was always asking me about what was happening with Optimus Prime or the Rebel Alliance? Why was he in such a rush to grow up if he wasn't tired of being a kid yet?

Mom and Dad had obviously had whatever talk they'd needed to have while we were outside, although Mom didn't really seem any more relaxed. I glanced sideways to catch Dad squeezing her shoulder in that way he did whenever she was too tense. She smiled at him in return.

"I think I'll go dig out those candles now," she said, more to get away from the news, I think, than out of any sense of urgency to prepare for another power outage.

"I need you two to behave tonight," Dad said to us after she left the room. "Your mom's under a lot of stress right now."

"I *am* behaving," said Pete, a little defensively.

"I didn't say you weren't," Dad replied. "I'm just telling you, okay?"

"Okay," we both agreed.

The big red BREAKING NEWS box still covered a third of the TV screen, but there didn't really seem to be anything breaking right at the moment. The dark skies had come and gone all over the world, a vast wave that seemed to have left few places unaffected. Now the same question was on everyone's mind: Just how many people *had* been lost? A thousand? Ten thousand? More?

The phone rang and Dad went to answer it even though Mom was yelling, "I'll get it!" as she hurried back up the stairs from the basement.

"I think it might be like a plague," said Pete. We were alone now in the living room. "Only instead of people getting sick, they're turning to glass."

"I don't think viruses can do that, Pete." I didn't care to consider the consequences of a wider spread. I didn't really want to think about any of it. I wanted to wind back the clock and have the whole day turn out differently. I'd even change the part about me landing my seedpod on the first try. It's not like I really got to enjoy my win anyway. I didn't even get my root beer float.

SIX

Mr. Crandall, as it turned out, wasn't the only victim in town.

Charlie Watts had turned to glass as well, while unloading stock in the back room of the Safeway store. He was twenty years old, a former junior hockey star who had just missed going pro. The Edmonton Oilers had actually drafted him in the fifth round when he was seventeen, but then a knee injury took him out for a year, and when he returned he just didn't have the moves that he used to. After a few unproductive months with the Oilers' farm team, he was forced to hang up his skates for good. It was a sad story that everyone in town knew well.

"Man," said Pete, shaking his head. "Talk about bad luck." I could tell that he was truly upset, maybe because he could sort of relate to Charlie—Pete played hockey, too—or maybe just because Charlie was still young and in his prime (aside from his knee problem); if people like him weren't safe, then who was?

The news quickly became a parade of arguing scientists and religious doom-and-gloom types, each with their own ideas about what was happening. They talked about random fluctuations in energy and matter and atmospheric anomalies; they threw around words like *revelations* and *rapture* and *reckoning*, as if anything serious that had to do with God must start with the letter *R*.

"That's it," Dad said finally, having obviously heard enough. "I'm shutting it off." And he did, even as Pete begged him not to.

"It's not even suppertime yet!" Pete complained. It was a rule in our house that the TV couldn't be on during supper. Mealtime was family time.

Dad checked his watch and then glanced sideways

at Mom. Truth be told, our regular suppertime had already come and gone.

Mom's eyes went suddenly wide at this realization. "Oh my God!" she said. "I completely forgot!"

Dad smiled. "Given the circumstances," he said, "I would have been more surprised if you'd remembered."

"Can we have hot dogs?" Pete asked hopefully. If Pete had his way, hot dogs would be on the menu every night of the week.

"Sure," said Dad. "Why not?"

Five minutes later Dad was standing outside in front of the barbecue with a package of all-beef franks. Lots of people in town preferred propane over briquettes, but Dad bucked the trend. The tradition of using charcoal was far more important to him than getting the meat cooked five minutes faster.

I watched as he rotated the dogs methodically, as if there were a prize for grilling them perfectly even all the way around. He was all concentration and didn't look up or over at me once.

When he was finished, we sat at the table and ate in silence. As usual, Pete took so long getting his buns ready with mustard, ketchup, and relish that his hot dogs must have been almost cold by the time he finally bit into them. I ate mine plain, without even really tasting them. I chewed and swallowed and thought about all those glass bodies.

"Everything's going to be fine," Dad assured me, as if he'd been reading my mind. That happened sometimes, or at least it seemed to. It was like we were both on the same wavelength or something, whereas Pete was always just a little out of tune.

"You've got crumbs in your beard," I told him. It happened every time Dad ate bread. Normally I waited for Mom to point it out to him, but this time I didn't. Maybe I was just trying to change the subject.

Pete kept looking at the black TV screen, as if willing it to come back on.

The phone rang again just as we were finishing eating. Mom answered, and then handed the phone over to Dad. It was Uncle Dean, checking in to see how we were doing.

"I'm going to go over there and get him," said Dad after he hung up a few minutes later. "I don't think he should be alone tonight."

Uncle Dean had never married. Mom said it was

because Dean wasn't attracted to the "marrying type," whatever that meant.

"Why doesn't he just drive over here himself?" Mom asked. "Why do you have to go?"

"He's already had a few beers," Dad replied. "He shouldn't be driving."

Mom sighed. "Fine," she said, "but no extra stops."

"I'll be back in a flash," Dad promised her.

As it happened, a flash was about fifteen minutes.

Pete and I sat waiting at the living room window, both of us spooked into silence by how quiet the neighborhood had become. Normally on a summer night like this one, there would be all sorts of noise, from lawn mowers and sprinklers to the constant shrieks and laughter of the Olson girls jumping rope or playing hopscotch down the way.

"It's like a ghost town," said Pete, and it really was, at least for a moment.

But then we saw movement, a pair of bikes coming down the street, each of them ridden by an identical slouching teen.

"The Messam twins," said Pete, his voice barely

more than a whisper, as if the schoolyard menaces might somehow hear him across the distance through the double-paned glass.

Instinctively, we both pulled back from the window, our fear of the mysterious glass plague momentarily replaced by a fear we'd shared since the twins first moved to Griever's Mill almost two years before.

The worst thing about the brothers was how random they could be in their bullying. There were times when Pete and I went weeks without either of them casting so much as a glance in our direction, but the minute we let our guards down and started feeling safe—*wham*—they were on us like gangbusters. It was the same for everyone they harassed. I think they fed off the kind of fear inspired by their own unpredictability. Mom said they had a sickness inside their souls.

I had no idea what the twins were doing out riding while everyone else was hunkered down with their families waiting for news, but whatever it was, it couldn't be good.

"Probably out looking for stuff to steal," said Pete. "While everyone is distracted."

I nodded and thought to myself that if the sky over Griever's Mill turned black a second time, karma should make the twins its next two victims. If only the universe worked that way.

Even after they'd ridden out of sight, we kept our distance from the window in case they circled the block and spotted us on a second pass. Eye contact alone was sometimes enough to get their evil gears turning. As it turned out, Dad and Uncle Dean got home before that could happen.

Uncle Dean came in wearing a casual smile and carrying an eighteen-pack of beer. He kicked off his boots and threw a glance at me and Pete, his gaze shifting sideways momentarily to the open curtain. "Zombie watch?" he asked.

"Something like that," said Pete.

"Well, I wouldn't worry if I were you," Uncle Dean replied with a wink. "I hear they only eat brains."

Pete scowled, but I could tell he was smiling underneath. It was exactly the sort of joke he would have made, if only he had thought of it first.

Just having Uncle Dean in the room was enough to

make me feel a little bit more at ease. It wasn't because he was always goofing around or cracking jokes (although he often was); it was more just the way he carried himself, as if he didn't have a care in the world.

He plopped himself down on the couch and uncapped a beer.

"So where are the circus clowns?" he asked, somehow managing to keep a straight face. "Your dad promised me circus clowns."

SEVEN

The neighborhood grew rowdy just before sunset, or at least a part of it did. This was nothing new, though; it happened almost every night now.

"Right on time," said Mom as a chorus of shrieks and jeers erupted out in our yard.

A band of blue jays had just arrived for their evening meal.

Blue jays are flashy birds—not just in the way they look, but also in the way they behave. From bullies and thieves to tricksters and helpers, there was no telling how the winged wonders might act from one day to the next. Sometimes they came to the feeders like a pack of wolves, crests raised and bristling with attitude, pretty much daring all the other birds to stand in their way, which few ever did. Other times they approached more cleverly, perfectly mimicking the call of a predator (usually a red-tailed hawk) in order to scare all the feeding birds away. The blue jays could then swoop in and eat in peace, at least for a moment or two, until the scattered birds got their confidence back. Still other times, the jays would perch in high branches above the feeders and appear to stand guard there, no longer imitating predators but actually watching for them and then sounding a genuine alarm if any appeared.

On this particular night, they were doing their wolf pack routine. I watched from the window as they came in at all angles, surrounding a particularly prized peanut canister as if it were a caribou separated from the rest of its herd, and scaring away a pair of white-breasted nuthatches in the process.

"Troublemakers," said Mom, standing beside me. She was smiling, though, amused at the band's antics.

That's what a group of blue jays is called: a "band." It makes sense, too, since jays are like rock stars out on the town, decked out in their finest blues, which, in reality, aren't even blues at all. Blue jay feathers are a trick. The pigment is actually brown. It's just the way that the cells in the feathers scatter light that gives them their false appearance.

I was surprised when I learned that. I guess some things you just take for granted, like what you see is what you get, even though it isn't always.

Dad used to say that you had to be careful about who and what you believed, because unlike blue jays, who only have one disguise and who only ever seem to lie for just one purpose, humans wear lots of different masks and tell all sorts of crazy stories for all sorts of crazy reasons, some of which might not even make a lick of sense.

"Just trust your gut," Dad would say. "It's the best BS meter you have."

I was reminded of all this as the sound of the jays outside converged with the sound of my dad scoffing at the TV screen.

"What a bunch of baloney," he said.

In addition to all the accounts of dark skies and mysterious transformations—"glassification," they were now calling it—some reporters were now talking to individuals who were claiming to have witnessed other strange phenomena as well, pretty much everything from ghosts and UFOs to spontaneous human combustion. None of it was confirmed, of course.

"They're really coming out of the woodwork now, aren't they?" said Uncle Dean.

"Who are?" asked Pete.

"The nutballs," said Dad. "They want their fifteen minutes."

"Well, let's not give it to them," said Mom. "Let's turn it off and do something else."

"Like what?" said Pete, who was still a bit sour about the loss of our computer. Uncle Dean had looked at it and declared it "pooched." He said it was hardware, not software.

"How about we play a game?" I suggested. A board game, I meant. We usually only played them on the weekends when Dad didn't have a bunch of paperwork to do, but since Uncle Dean was over and the whole world appeared to be going crazy, I figured that maybe we could break from routine. We could definitely all do with a break from reality.

Pete immediately nominated Risk, but since Mom was going to be playing and didn't appreciate that game, Dad overruled him and picked Monopoly instead, which was okay by me since I sometimes actually won at that one. I went upstairs to grab the box from the closet, and a few minutes later we were on our way.

"I call top hat," said Pete, predictably. He was the only one who ever wanted to play with that piece, but for some reason he always felt the need to claim it.

Uncle Dean grabbed the car, while Mom picked the thimble and Dad the wheelbarrow, which left only me, still hemming and hawing over what I felt like using. Sometimes I picked the dog or the boot, but I liked the iron as well, not because of what it was, but simply because it had a nice streamlined look to it. Today I took the boot.

It felt weird to be setting up for a game considering what we knew and what was happening. It almost felt *wrong*. But what were we supposed to do? It wasn't as if we'd been given any instructions—like if your house is on fire and you need to get out, stay low to the floor where the smoke is thinnest, or if you're outside and there's lightning, don't lean up against a tree because if it gets struck, the current could run straight through the trunk and into you.

All we could really do was just wait, and if you're going to be waiting anyway, you might as well be rolling dice and buying up real estate.

As always, Pete ignored all the lower-priced properties and tried only for the ritzy ones like Marvin Gardens, Pennsylvania Avenue, and Boardwalk. It was a strategy that only ever worked if he got lucky on his first few trips around the board, but for some reason, he remained committed to it.

I was more of a buy-anything-and-put-up-houses-as-fast-as-you-can type player, which had its own risks but seemed more sensible overall.

On this particular occasion, I managed to scoop up all the red properties in only four circuits, this while Pete repeatedly landed on Chance or Luxury Tax, which had him shaking his head and scoffing as if the will of the universe had been bent against him.

"You could have bought railroads," I reminded him. He'd landed on at least two of them.

"So?" he said. "Who the heck wants railroads? You can't even put hotels on them."

I just shrugged. I thought the railroads were great, if only just because they provided you with safe landing areas when you owned them.

"Woo-hoo!" said Uncle Dean with exaggerated excitement as he passed Go and landed on Baltic Avenue. "A biker bar to go with my bowling alley!" He'd purchased Mediterranean Avenue just a few turns before.

"You're on the fast track to high society," said Dad with a laugh.

"The Hamptons, here I come!" Uncle Dean replied. Mom laughed then, too, and I had to smile, even though I didn't really get what the joke was.

The game continued, and it wasn't long before houses and hotels sprang up all over the place. I wasn't doing well. My red properties were keeping me afloat, but I hadn't managed to get a set of anything else. I was faring better than Pete, though. In a desperate bid to stay alive, he ended up trading away two yellow properties so that he had Park Place and Boardwalk both. But it was too little too late; when next he landed on Pacific, Mom cleaned him right out.

I braced myself for the usual complaints and excuses, everything from dumb rules or accounting errors to unlucky rolls of the dice. Pete was a sore loser, no matter what the game, so I knew it had to be coming. Or at least I *thought* it had to be coming.

As it happened, something else came first. Or, rather, something else *went*, namely our power. One second Pete was scowling down at the game board, deconstructing how it all went wrong, and the next he was saying "Oh crap..." into the darkness.

EIGHT

The sun had long since set, so it wasn't just dark; it was pitch-black. It immediately came to mind that if anyone in the room turned to glass, none of us would even see it happening. I started to freak out a little at the thought. My chest felt tight and my heart began to pound. That's when it started: a low rumbling outside. A second later there was a flash, followed by more rumbling, closer now.

"Oh, thank God!" said Mom, and then she laughed, a half-nervous, half-relieved sound.

Only then did it occur to me that we'd lost power simply because it was storming.

Pete and I both went to the window while Mom lit a candle. It was starting to rain now, and the wind had picked up so much that the suet feeders were swinging like wrecking balls on their branches. There were no birds out there at this hour, of course. They were all off sleeping wherever it was that birds went to sleep.

"I knew it was going to storm," said Pete.

The rain intensified for a moment before turning to hail, pea sized at first, but then marbles. The sound of it clattering off the porcelain birdbath near the front step reminded me of a similar storm we'd had the year before, and how Pete and I had run outside in our rubber boots with green plastic army helmets strapped to our heads, the hail becoming shrapnel from enemy fire, ferocious and deafening, and satisfying in a way that only maybe boys could really appreciate.

I remembered how we'd danced around like idiots on the front lawn, with Mom and Dad smiling and shaking their heads at us from just inside the front door.

That particular barrage had lasted only a few

minutes, after which the sun climbed out from its bunker and crowned off the day with a rainbow so crisp and perfect that it might have been drawn and colored against the sky with some giant crayons and a mammoth protractor.

There would be no rainbow tonight, but I smiled at the memory all the same.

Uncle Dean turned his attention back to his slew of properties and his huge stacks of cash. He rubbed his hands together and grinned, looking altogether villainous in the candlelight. "Should we put the final nail in this coffin, or what?" he said.

Our arms cast long shadows across the board, and the dice seemed somehow bigger now, more substantial. I felt strangely intimidated at the thought of picking them up, of rolling them, as if the numbers that fell would determine more than just my fate in the game. Not that my fate in the game was in any doubt. Dad and I were pretty much toast.

"Not so fast, buster," Mom replied. "Nobody's nailing anything shut just yet."

And so it went on, the skies outside still rumbling and dumping rain as the car and the thimble went head-to-head. Ultimately the thimble would triumph, but Mom, being Mom, only smiled in her soft sort of way.

Uncle Dean glowered in mock disgust. "Robbed, I tell you! I was robbed!"

"As if!" Pete quickly chimed in. "You were the banker! Just admit it, Mom kicked your butt!" I think he only stuck around until the end to gloat on Mom's behalf.

"Fine," Uncle Dean finally relented. "She kicked my butt." He tipped his hat in Mom's direction and then spent the next few minutes adjusting it and readjusting it on his head.

As always, Mom and I did the cleanup, with her putting all the cards and pieces away while I sorted out the play money. Dad waited until we were finished and then announced that it was high time for Pete and me to head off to bed, which it was, although I wasn't really tired.

"But it's still storming outside," Pete complained.

"Take a candle with you," Dad replied.

"But don't set it near your curtains," Mom added. "And blow it out before you lie down."

"Fine," said Pete. He picked out the biggest and

brightest of the candles that were already burning and led the way upstairs, but not before Uncle Dean warned us about watching for bogeymen. He had his own candle held up to his face, like a camp counselor with an upturned flashlight, planting seeds of fear in the darkness.

Pete and I shared a room, but we each had our own side, the dividing line clearly marked by a long piece of duct tape that ran the length of the faded blue carpet. The walls on Pete's half were covered with sports memorabilia and photos of hot rods that he had clipped out from various car magazines—probably ones he'd gotten from the library and shouldn't have taken scissors to. My walls held only pictures of animals, the prize of the bunch being a big eagle poster that I'd won in a dart-throwing game at the fair in Paulson.

Ten minutes after getting to our room, I was in my pajamas and under my covers. Not Pete, though.

"What are you doing?" I asked him.

He had the candleholder in one hand and was quietly rummaging through the closet with the other.

"I need some batteries for the radio," he said.

I almost told him just to plug the radio in, but then I remembered that we had a candle burning for a reason.

It took a few minutes, but Pete finally managed to dig out four AAs, two from a remote-controlled jeep, and two from the remote itself.

"Bingo," Pete said. He loaded them into the radio and turned the knob. There was a click, and then nothing.

"Dead," I said.

"Uh-uh," Pete disagreed. "Just listen."

I aimed an ear in his direction and tried to hear past the patter of rain on the roof and against our window-pane, and sure enough, there it was: static. It was so faint that I thought the radio's volume must be turned almost all the way down, but Pete shook his head when I asked him.

"I think the speaker's blown," he told me, at which point he lifted the radio up onto his shoulder and pressed its single speaker right to his ear. He turned the dial to search for a signal. A minute or two went by.

"Anything yet?" I asked him. The candle now sat on the dresser between our two beds, but I was pretty much ready to blow it out. I was tired and wanted the day to be over. Maybe tomorrow would be normal, aside from the fact that everyone would still be talking about how odd today had been.

"Shh," Pete told me, which I guess meant no. He then grumbled a little in growing frustration, which turned out to be the last sound I heard before I finally gave up and closed my eyes.

The first shatterings happened a few hours later, while most of our town was sleeping. Most, but not all.

NINE

Get up!" whispered Pete, shaking me. "C'mon, get up!"

I groaned and rolled over, looked at him through squinted eyes. "Why?"

"Something's happening," he said. "Get dressed."

"What time is it?" I asked him. I could hear the alarm in his voice but it wasn't quite registering yet. My brain was still partially trapped in a dream about small glass houses and huge black dice. The dice had been tumbling down a mountainside, flashing random numbers as they picked up speed.

"Never mind that!" said Pete. "Just get up!"

I glanced at the window and saw that it was just beginning to get light outside, which meant that it was probably around five a.m. I sat up, a sinking feeling settling into the pit of my stomach as a thought occurred to me, an explanation for why my older brother was being so serious so early in the morning.

"Are they okay?" I said. "Did it happen again?"

"Who?" he asked me, giving me a look of confused impatience.

"Mom and Dad," I said. "Uncle Dean."

"They're fine," he said dismissively, but there was a pause, as if he wasn't completely certain but was just assuming they were.

"Did you check?" I asked.

He shook his head. "No, it's not that. It's something else."

"What is?"

He huffed, like I was purposely making things difficult.

"Just tell me," I said.

"It's old man Crandall," he replied. "And Charlie. I think they might have shattered."

I stared at him, not understanding.

"I heard it on the radio," he tried to explain. "They said it's happening all over, to the ones who turned. They're going to pieces."

"Pieces?"

"Pieces."

I tried to imagine what that would look like, a person coming apart in the way that Pete was suggesting. There one second and then not, a man-turned-statue reduced to mere fragments upon the floor, a mess to be swept up like a dropped cup or plate. It was hard to picture. Impossible, really.

"How?" I asked.

He shook his head. "I don't know. Just suddenly, they're saying."

"All of them?"

"Uh-uh, just some. Hurry up and get dressed."

I sat there for a moment, blinking and wondering what the world was coming to, where it was heading. Pete went to the window and stood there waiting for me, although what exactly he was waiting for, I wasn't sure. It wasn't like there was anything we could do that required jeans instead of pajamas.

Nevertheless, I reached down to the floor for yesterday's Levi's, thinking they were probably still clean enough to wear again. There was something sticking out of one of the back pockets, flat and square and white along its edges: Mr. Crandall's Polaroid photo. I'd completely forgotten about it.

I took it out to have a look, expecting to see an image of Main Street, shadowed by the strange dark mass that had temporarily blanketed the sky. What I saw instead was the very same blur that had been in the photo the day before, when I thought it wasn't fully developed yet. Obviously it had to be by now.

I squinted my eyes and brought the photo closer, realizing only now that the dark blur had a depth and shape to it, sort of humanoid but featureless. A body of smoke and heat shimmer, hovering, it seemed, like an angel or a ghost...not *of* this world, but somehow in it, at least for the split second that the camera's shutter would have been open. An icy shiver ran through me, followed by a strong compulsion to hurl the photo away or, better yet, destroy it. But first I had to make sure that what I was seeing was actually there, that my eyes and my mind weren't playing tricks on me.

"Pete!" I whispered. "Come look at this."

He turned around and raised an eyebrow at me.

"It's the photo," I told him. "From yesterday."

"What about it?" he asked while stepping forward and reaching out for it.

He took it before I could answer, before I could even think of *how* to answer.

He pursed his lips and cocked his head a little, and then his face went suddenly pale. He let go of the photo so fast it was as if he'd been burned, but even as it fell to the carpet, his eyes never left it.

"What do you think it might be?" I asked him, even though I knew that the best he could do—the best *either* of us could do—was simply guess. One thing, however, seemed clear to me: Whatever the blur might be, it was probably the last thing that old man Crandall saw before he turned to glass.

Pete shook his head. "I don't know, but it couldn't have been there when the photo was taken. We would have seen it."

"What if it just blinked in and out?" I said. "Like that—" I snapped my fingers.

He considered. "Maybe." He flipped the photo over with his toe, as if worried that the blurred being might somehow escape. Maybe we would turn to glass then as well, me on the edge of my bed and Pete on the middle of our floor, a pair of preteen statues that Mom would eventually walk in on. I could just imagine how bad she'd freak out.

"We should burn it," I said, looking down at it. "Just in case."

"Definitely," Pete agreed. "Let's take it downstairs to the fireplace."

I nodded. "You can carry it," I told him.

"Uh-uh, no way. You brought it home. You carry it."

"Rock, paper, scissors," I replied.

Pete stared at me for a second. "Fine. On three."

We counted together, hands poised. "One, two, three..."

Rock. Rock.

"Again," we said simultaneously. "One, two, three..."

I knew from past experience that Pete rarely picked

paper, and that he wasn't likely to pick the same thing twice in a row, so I stuck with my closed fist.

"Rock breaks scissors," I said.

"Best of three," he said.

"Fat chance. You take it down and I'll get dressed."

"Fine," he said. "But I'm using your ball glove. . . ."

TEN

I thought it would only take a minute and that Mom and Dad would never be the wiser, but as it turns out, Polaroid photos and fire don't mix. Something to do with the chemicals, I guess.

"Whoa!" said Pete, waving his hand in front of his nose. He took a step back, which probably wasn't far enough.

"Don't breathe it in," I told him. "It might be toxic." Taking my own advice, I closed my mouth and waited for the fire to finish the snapshot off, all the while thinking that it was taking far too long, and that the noxious smoke was sure to make its way up the stairs and under the door of our parents' bedroom.

But aside from that worry, I was glad to see it burning, glad to know that no one else would have to see what Pete and I already had, especially Mom, who might decide that the strange dark blur was a demon or something...which maybe it was. Maybe the terrible stench wasn't chemical at all. Maybe it was brimstone.

The photo shriveled, blackened, and finally dissolved into ash. My eyes continued to water from the harsh fumes. I wondered belatedly if the photo might have been one of a kind, and if we might have just watched a crucial clue to the global mystery go up in smoke.

"Maybe we should've just buried it," I said.

Pete gave a small nod of agreement. "Maybe," he said, and then his head turned quickly sideways, as if he'd heard something, perhaps Mom's or Dad's feet hitting the floor upstairs, or maybe just their voices.

"What?"

"Shh," he said, still listening.

I didn't hear anything, but my first reaction was to get back upstairs and into bed. I would have, too, if Pete hadn't stopped me.

"Just wait," he told me. "I wanna check something." He reached out and turned on the TV.

Normally, it would have been strange to think that anyone was even reporting the news at this time of day, let alone watching it, but I guess the glass plague had finally made round-the-clock coverage useful. And Pete had been right—something *was* happening.

I listened for details about the so-called shatterings, but what I heard instead was the sound of Dad's voice, booming at us as he came down the stairs in his sweatpants and muscle shirt, his hair flat on one side of his head and sticking up on the other.

"What in God's name are you two burning at five o'clock in the morning?"

"Nothing anymore," Pete replied, which, although true, wasn't at all the right answer.

"A photo," I quickly chimed in, figuring it was wisest to come clean before Pete made things any worse. "A Polaroid photo. Mr. Crandall took it, just before he turned into a statue. I had it in my back pocket, but then I forgot about it...."

Dad narrowed his eyes, clearly not following.

"There was something in the photo," Pete explained.

"A weird dark thing. Ben freaked out when he saw it, so we came down to burn it."

"It wasn't just me," I said, glaring at Pete now. "You were freaking out, too."

Dad shushed us. "What do you mean, a weird dark thing?"

"A blurry figure," I told him. "Dark and blurry, like a ghost."

"It didn't have a face," Pete added, a fact that Dad appeared relieved to hear.

"Those photos don't always expose properly," he said, his anger dissipating now. "Sometimes there are dark spots, blotches."

I immediately shook my head. I'd seen the kind of photos that Dad meant, the ones that got messed up during development. "Uh-uh," I said. "It wasn't like that. Something was there on the street when it happened."

"But nobody saw it?" asked Dad. "Even though everyone was looking outside?"

"It might have only been there for a second," I said. "Like a split second." I looked to Pete, thinking he'd back me up, but he didn't.

"Maybe Dad's right," he said. "Maybe it *was* just a splotch."

I stared at him. "What are you talking about? You *saw* it."

"I saw *something*," he admitted, "but maybe it wasn't what we thought it was. Maybe we didn't look close enough."

"You wouldn't even touch it! You had to use my ball glove to pick it up!" He was actually still wearing the glove. He pulled it off as soon as I mentioned it, as if he'd never needed it at all and had only been playing along, humoring his little brother. I felt like punching him.

"And why the hell is the TV on?" Dad continued, his hand reaching for the remote control.

"Wait!" said Pete. "People are shattering!"

Dad hesitated, his eyes on the screen now instead of on us, his expression changing as what he was seeing began to sink in. "Shattering?" he said. "What the...?"

"Maybe we should go and check on old man Crandall," Pete suggested. "Make sure that he's okay. Mrs. Crandall, too."

I understood then why Pete had flip-flopped on me

so quickly, and why he'd told me to get dressed in the first place. He'd already been thinking ahead, planning to wake up Dad to tell him the news, his assumption being that Dad would probably hop in his truck and drive to the general store to find out if the petrified old man was now just a pile on the floor. If we were lucky (and if we were already up and dressed and ready to go), Dad might take us with him.

The dark shape in the photo really *had* scared Pete as much as it had scared me, but now that the photo was gone, it no longer mattered. Best to just forget it and return to the plan.

Pete should have known better, though. It wasn't as if Dad ever let us tag along to any of the accident scenes that he went to as a first responder. Why would this be any different?

"*We* aren't going anywhere," Dad said. "You two shouldn't even be out of bed, never mind starting fires and watching TV. Now, get upstairs and back in your room, and stay there until I say otherwise. Got it?"

He was using his firm voice, but there was a shakiness in it that normally wasn't there.

"Got it," I said, but Pete wasn't giving up so easily.

"Are *you* gonna go to the general store?" he asked Dad.

"Never mind what I'm going to do. Just get up to your room like I told you to, before I decide to ground you."

"You might as well ground us anyway," Pete stubbornly continued. "It's not as if Mom is going to let us go outside."

"I'm not going to stand here arguing with you," Dad warned him. That's when Mom appeared at the foot of the stairs.

"Is everything all right?" she asked, her forest-green house coat wrapped tight around her and her feet in her favorite slippers, the ones with fake fur around the edges. (Mom wouldn't have worn them if the fur were real.)

"Everything's fine," Dad assured her. He reached out and turned off the TV. "The boys couldn't sleep, so they came downstairs."

"What's that smell?" Mom asked.

The burned-photo stench had lessened a bit but was definitely still in the air.

"Just a bit of mischief," Dad explained, without really explaining at all. "Nothing to worry about." He looked at us each in turn then, his expression making it clear that we weren't to mention the photo.

For a second, I thought Pete would anyway, just to make things difficult, but thankfully he bit his tongue. Until we got to our room, that is, at which point he blew up about how unfair it all was and how he shouldn't be treated like a kid anymore. He was twelve going on thirteen, practically a *teenager.*

I wasn't really worried about what was or wasn't fair. And I didn't feel like I needed to see for myself whether old man Crandall had gone to pieces or not either. What good would it do us?

Pete stopped pacing and went to the window, where he stood for ten minutes, until Dad got in his truck and backed out of the driveway.

"I knew it," he said.

"Why do you even *want* to go?" I asked. I wished that he'd never woken me up in the first place. If I'd slept a little bit later, things might have turned out differently. I might have put on clean jeans instead of yesterday's pair. The photo might have gotten ruined in the wash before I ever even looked at it. But now, instead, I couldn't stop thinking about it, and wondering...

"Just because" was Pete's only reply, which didn't tell me anything but was basically the answer that I expected. Pete always acted on impulses. If you told him there was a haunted house on the corner, he'd be over there before anyone could say "boo," even though he might not be able to say exactly *why* he wanted to see a ghost.

But just because "just because" was good enough for Pete, that didn't mean it was good enough for me.

"That's not an answer," I told him. "The sky's not blue *just because*. Water's not wet *just because*."

"Why is it wet, then?" he asked me.

"What? I don't know, because of its molecular structure, I guess. But that's not the point."

"It is, though," he disagreed. "Why is the molecular structure the way it is?"

"Because that's how the atoms are arranged," I answered, digging deep into science class memories.

"And why are the atoms arranged that way?"

"Nobody knows *that*."

"Exactly," he said. "Just because. It's the answer to everything."

"That's stupid," I told him, even though there was something weirdly true about his logic. Maybe I was wrong in believing that Pete never thought deeply about things. Maybe sometimes he did, only it didn't bother him that there might not be any real answers. He could accept that. I couldn't.

He just shrugged and left it at that, abandoning his spot at the window for a spot on the floor. He sat back against the side of his bed and lifted the half-broken radio up to his shoulder, pressing the speaker against his ear.

ELEVEN

George Crandall was still in one piece. So was Charlie Watts at the Safeway store. Hundreds of others around the world weren't, though. Thousands maybe. Nobody really knew for sure yet. Scientists were analyzing some of the fragments, using microscopes and spectrometers. They weren't saying much, other than that the substance wasn't actually glass. It might look like glass and shatter like glass, but apparently it was "compositionally unique." It didn't matter. People were still calling it glass.

Dad was talking about going out for a while. He said he had a stack of papers that he needed to drop off in Paulson, which was where the insurance company that he worked for had its office. Paulson was a large town about thirty minutes south of Griever's Mill. There was a big mall there and three grocery stores instead of just the one that we had. There were a number of restaurants, too, including a Venice House that had the absolute best pepperoni pizza. Just thinking about it made my mouth water.

"You can't just go to work like it's a normal day," said Mom. She was ignoring the fact that, had it been a normal day, Dad would have left at seven a.m., and now it was an hour past lunchtime.

"I need to get paid," Dad told her. "Plus I should grab a few things, groceries and whatnot, before too many others get the same idea." There had been reports on the news about panicked shopping, with people buying generators and stocking up on canned goods.

"Paulson's got that outfitter place, too," said Uncle Dean. "Might be worthwhile stopping there." He and Dad were both sitting at the dining room table, with

Mom looking at them from the kitchen. I was on the floor in the living room, in front of the TV, which I had muted at Dad's request.

"Don't encourage him," Mom told Uncle Dean.

Uncle Dean said sorry and went back to nursing his coffee. His baseball cap was sitting a little askew today, and his eyes were noticeably bloodshot, which was explained by all the empty beer bottles in the case by the door.

"I have to stop at the drugstore as well," said Dad, giving Mom a look that said, *Remember?*

"Oh, right," Mom replied with a sigh. "I totally forgot."

The drugstore in Paulson was where Mom got her anxiety medication. I knew that because it said PAULSON PHARMACY right on the bottle. I'd wondered at first why she didn't just get the prescription filled at the local Safeway, but I guess she was worried that someone might talk, that it might get out that she was on "happy pills." People wouldn't understand, and when people don't understand things, they usually criticize them, like the way Pete always criticized me for liking birds.

“I can hang around here until you get back,” Uncle Dean offered.

“Would you?” said Dad.

Uncle Dean shrugged. “Sure, why not?”

Mom wasn’t satisfied, though. “What if something happens while you’re driving?” she said.

“I guess I’ll pull over,” Dad replied.

“What if you can’t pull over?” Mom pressed. She was standing right next to the table now, her arms crossed.

“Now you’re just being paranoid,” Dad told her.

“You don’t know what’s going to happen. Nobody does.”

“Fine,” said Dad. “I’ll take Ben with me. I could use some help with the groceries anyway.”

“What about Pete?” I asked, while trying to avoid thinking about having to take the wheel if Dad were to suddenly glassify right beside me.

“Let him sleep,” said Mom. “He needs it.”

Pete had stayed up right through the night and into the morning. He finally fell asleep with the radio still against his ear, a lullaby of static and whispered news bits. I switched it off to save the batteries, though

I doubted that Pete would thank me for it later, especially once he discovered that Dad had gone off to Paulson and had taken me along with him. Pete would be annoyed. I could pretty much count on that.

"All right, then," said Dad. "I guess we might as well get a move on. You ready, champ?" he asked me. "Hit the head if you need to."

I didn't need to, so I got my shoes on.

"Drive carefully," Mom said as we were leaving. "And hurry back, please."

Dad promised we would.

TWELVE

The closer we got to Paulson, the better Dad's radio came in. The crackling voices gave way to clear speech, although it might have been better if they hadn't. We soon discovered that new glass storms were spreading out all over the east.

Portsmouth, New Hampshire, had gone totally dark, and so had Bangor, Maine, along with half the state of Vermont. The shatterings continued as well, just a few at a time, here and there. Always, they said, without any precursor.

I shifted around in my seat to look in every direction,

but aside from some typical summer clouds—a few small cumulous islands connected by wisps—the sky held no trace of malice. Even so, a ball of dread began to build in the pit of my stomach.

"Should we go back?" I asked Dad.

He shook his head. "No point now. We're almost there."

I could already see the outskirts of Paulson in the distance. We passed the small airport a moment later, and then the farm equipment dealership, where huge combines and tractors sat in a row along the road's edge, some of their tires twice as tall as I was.

"We'll be fine," Dad tried to reassure me. "It's a good thing we left when we did, though. Your mother would have taken my keys." He smiled as he said this, but it didn't quite reach his eyes.

We stopped at the office first, and then the pharmacy, which was right across the street from the huge IGA supermarket.

"We'll just park here and walk over," said Dad. "Looks like we're going to be in for a bit of an adventure."

I was going to ask why, but then I noticed the state of the parking lot, not just the number of cars there (lots), but also the number of shopping carts left out in the open instead of being put back in the cart corral. Usually there were a few of them left abandoned—Dad always pointed them out as an example of how lazy people had become—but today there were dozens of them, sitting this way and that all over the place, as if people just couldn't get out of there fast enough.

"Unbelievable," said Dad.

It actually wasn't too bad inside. People were moving quickly and you could feel the tension in the air, but nobody was being rude or pushy or trying to leave the store without paying, which probably wouldn't have surprised me considering how long the checkout lines were.

Dad said that we were lucky Paulson was just a big town and not a big city, where people probably wouldn't be behaving so calmly.

The canned food section had been hit pretty hard. Most of the good soups were already gone, so we were left choosing among three types of chowder. We ended up grabbing a case of each and got lucky in finding some vegetable beef barley tucked in the back. We grabbed three bags of rice and some SPAM and canned tuna as well, and then just some regular groceries, too—crackers and cereal and whatnot. Also birdseed—I made sure to remember the birdseed.

Dad tried to call Mom twice on his cell phone to let her know that we were okay and that we'd be leaving Paulson after one more stop, but both times the call got dropped before he could talk to her. He swore and dug a quarter out of his pocket. "Here," he said. "Go find a pay phone while I get this stuff. I think there's an old one near the bus stop around the corner—if it still works."

Mom must have been waiting right by the phone, because she answered on the first ring. "Tell your father to get his butt in gear," she said, which I repeated verbatim, with a slight smile, when I rejoined Dad.

"I didn't realize it had been out of gear," he said.

Ten minutes later we were on our way, our cart left neatly in the corral. We didn't go straight home, though. Dad wanted to check out the outfitter place that Uncle Dean had mentioned.

It was a lot quieter there. I only counted eight people other than me and Dad.

From what we ended up buying, you'd have thought

we were going on a giant camping trip or something. We got kerosene, new lanterns, four big sleeping bags, and even a giant box of army-style food, which was basically just little packages that you could heat up by pouring some water—cold water, even—into the bag. Dad said it worked by chemical reaction.

I thought it might be interesting to try one out, but was also hoping that we wouldn't have to. If it got to the point where we *needed* the ration packs, then it would probably mean things had gotten real bad.

"Hope for the best but prepare for the worst, eh?" said the guy at the counter.

"Words to live by," Dad replied. "Words to live by."

We picked up our bags and made for the exit. That's when the air raid siren sounded.

I stopped dead in my tracks as the low wail built up in intensity, like a thrum that starts outside your body and then vibrates its way right in, until you're hearing it more with your bones than you are with your ears.

I hadn't even known that Paulson *had* an air raid siren. I guess they probably just used it for tornado warnings.

Dad didn't realize that I'd stopped, and continued

right out the door. The guy who rang up our stuff came out from behind the counter and ran outside as well, eager to see what was happening. Clearly it wasn't a tornado. A regular storm wouldn't have had time to brew up in the fifteen minutes we'd been in the store.

Dad poked his head back in a second later, his eyes full of alarm. "We need to leave, Ben," he said. "*Now.*"

My feet came unglued from the floor, but I only got a few steps outside before stopping once again. The siren was almost deafening. The sky to the south was alive with a dark churning mass that dwarfed the one Pete and I had seen from the roof of Uncle Dean's garage. It was moving faster than that one as well, not so much gliding as billowing forward like one of those pyroclastic clouds that come from volcanoes. It was terrifying and mesmerizing all at once.

Dad yelled at me to get moving, his voice stretched and dampened, like I was hearing it from under water, in slow motion.

I don't really remember throwing my bags in the back of the truck or climbing into the passenger seat, but I obviously did, and before I knew it we were back on the highway, speeding north.

"You okay?" Dad was asking me.

As quick as it hit me, my adrenaline seemed to evaporate. I nodded, then glanced at the side-view mirror, then looked away, not liking what I found there. Instead I focused on the power poles in the ditch, my eyes tracing the drooping wires from one to the next. Some of the poles had white stains near their tops from bird poop. Hawk poop, to be specific. They liked to perch on the poles in the daytime, watching for rodents in the fields and ditches.

I decided to do a count to distract myself. I often did them anyway. The most I'd ever seen between Paulson and home was sixteen—a mix of red-tailed and Swainson's hawks. I liked the Swainson's better because they weren't skittish—you could stop and watch them without them flying away, whereas the red-tails almost always took off as soon as you began to slow down.

"I don't see it anymore," said Dad a few minutes later. "I think we're in the clear." He didn't slow down, though. Nor did he turn the radio back on.

I kept on counting.

Crows and ravens were usually common on the poles as well, maybe even more so than the hawks, but not today. By the time we reached the Griever's Mill turnoff, I'd counted seven red-tails and six Swainson's, but not a single raven or crow. I wondered where they all were, and whether their absence meant something. I couldn't imagine what.

THIRTEEN

Mom was totally freaking out by the time we got home. Apparently, the whole town was. Lots of people had friends and family in Paulson, so word had gotten out quick that something was happening, although nobody had any details since Paulson's phones had all gone dead just moments after the darkness swept in.

"Should we even stay here?" Mom asked Dad. "Is it safe?"

Dad told her we'd have to sit tight and just wait and see. We could leave in a hurry if we needed to.

"And go where?" she asked him.

"Wherever we need to," Dad replied.

"I've got jerry cans at the garage," said Uncle Dean. "I should go fill them right now, while I still can."

Griever's Mill only had two gas stations. If all of a sudden everyone decided to leave, they would probably both be backed up down the block.

"I'll grab my generator, too," Uncle Dean added.

But first he'd have to get back to his house to grab his truck, which meant driving him over there.

"We'll all go together," Mom decided, and so we did, with Uncle Dean riding in the bed of the truck like a farm dog, surrounded by bags and boxes. The sky was blue and white and holding steady, at least for now.

We dropped him off and headed back home. Dad took Mom inside and told me and Pete to unload the truck, except for the camping gear. He told us to leave that for now.

"How bad was it?" Pete asked me. "In Paulson?"

It was the first chance we'd had to talk on our own since I got back.

"Bad," I told him. "It was way bigger this time. And Paulson has an air raid siren. Did you know that?"

Pete nodded. "I knew that. You should've woken me up. I would've woken *you* up."

"Mom told me not to," I replied, as if that had been the sole determining factor.

"Did it look different at all?" he asked me.

"Different how?"

"I don't know, just different."

"It was scarier than the first time," I told him. "Faster, too."

"So it's getting stronger, then, whatever it is."

I shrugged.

"Maybe next time it'll stay," Pete went on. "Maybe it'll be dark forever."

"I doubt it, Pete."

He ignored me. "The crops will die first, and then the animals, and then us. Unless we're all glass or shattered by that time. Then it won't matter."

"That won't happen."

"Why not?" he asked.

"It just won't," I told him. It couldn't.

Pete picked up one of the cases of soup cans and made a face. "Chowder?"

"Most of the good stuff was gone."

"Already?"

I shrugged again.

"I hate chowder," he complained.

"Me too," I said.

We took the stuff inside.

An hour went by, and still we had power and light. Dad talked to somebody over the phone, probably one of the farmers he sold insurance to. When he got off he said that Paulson was in the clear now, and that the glass storm had apparently veered off east before unraveling.

That was the word he used: *unraveling*. I imagined the darkness coming untangled like so many dark threads from a ball.

Mom breathed a sigh of relief. Pete seemed strangely disappointed.

"I just wanted to see it," he explained. "I didn't want it to go right over us or anything."

Uncle Dean returned with only a single jerry can, his jaw clenched in anger.

"What's wrong?" Dad asked him.

"Someone broke into my shop last night," he said. "Took the generator and some of my tools. Only left me with one bloody jerry can. Busted into my pop machine as well."

"What?" said Dad. "Are you kidding me? Did you report it to Wayne yet?" Constable Wayne Sheery, he meant. Dad and Uncle Dean were both friends with him, and he came over sometimes for coffee or barbecues.

Uncle Dean nodded. "Doubt it'll do me much good, though."

"Who on earth would do such a thing?" Mom asked, at which point Pete and I shared a look, our minds both zeroing in on a pair of identical faces. Pete turned to Uncle Dean.

"Lester and Lars," he said. "I bet it was them."

Dad started to say something about how we had to be careful when it came to throwing around accusations, but Uncle Dean narrowed his eyes and said, "The Messam boys? Why would you say that?"

"We saw them last night on their bikes," said Pete. "Riding around."

"When?" asked Uncle Dean.

"When Dad went to pick you up."

Uncle Dean turned to Dad. "They might have seen

me in your truck. If they did, they would've known that I wouldn't be at home."

Uncle Dean didn't just work at the shop; he lived there, too, in a tiny low-ceilinged apartment right above it.

"Possibly," Dad admitted. "Still, we can't just go over there and start pointing fingers. James is liable to point something back at us if we do."

A gun, he meant. James Messam was ex-army, and a drinker, too.

"That man is dangerous," said Mom. "Just leave it to Wayne."

"There's nothing Wayne can do," Uncle Dean replied. "Two boys riding their bikes isn't exactly evidence."

"No," Dad agreed. "It isn't. It could've been someone else, too. We don't know for sure."

Pete was convinced, though. Later that night he looked at me and said, "We can't just let them get away with it. They already get away with everything."

I almost asked him what we could do, but then I stopped myself. I was scared that he might have an answer.

FOURTEEN

The next day brought with it more blackouts and more shattered bodies, but not much new in the way of actual information. Griever's Mill escaped being hit again, and Paulson was spared this time, too, although the impact from yesterday's storm was still being felt by everyone there. Sixteen people had turned to glass, with two of them shattering just a few hours later. The rest remained intact.

Politicians made more speeches, asking everyone to please remain calm, to keep the peace and trust that those in charge would get to the bottom of things, to which Dad scoffed. "That'll be the day, when I put my trust in a politician."

Uncle Dean went down to the police station to do a follow-up and to give a full account of everything that had been taken in the break-in. He mentioned the Messams while he was there, but was told that there probably wasn't much to be done without any proof. Constable Sheery said he could talk to the twins, but that was it. He couldn't even look around their property without a warrant. His hands were pretty much tied.

"Fat load of good just talking to them is going to do," said Pete. He was sweating and breathing hard from swinging an ax.

Dad had given us the task of building up the woodpile alongside the garage. I think he thought if he kept us busy, we'd worry less about what was going on. But for me it had the opposite effect. It wasn't just the glass plague that I had to worry about now, but also the possibility of accidentally hacking off my toes. Not that that was likely to happen with Pete doing all the work, mind you. I offered to take a turn, but he said he was fine. I could tell that the gears were turning inside his brain.

He set another log up on the cutting block and gave it a whack, catching only the edge this time instead of the center. A splinter of bark went flying into the garage wall and almost hit me on the way by, while the rest of the log tipped sideways off the block. It was a lazy swing. Pete was getting tired.

"Gimme that," I said.

He ignored me, and instead just put the head of the ax to the ground, leaning his weight on the handle.

"We're gonna have to get it back ourselves," he told me.

"What?" I asked him. "The generator? Are you crazy?"

"We'll need it if the power goes out for good."

"Who says it's gonna go out for good?"

"Nobody," he replied. "But it might. The guy on the radio says it's possible."

I rolled my eyes. "As if he'd know. He's just a reporter."

Pete shook his head. "I don't think so. Not this guy."

He explained that he'd found a new station, one that he hadn't been able to tune in to before. Apparently it was just one person talking, mostly about the glass plague.

"You can tell he's smart," said Pete. "And not just smart like a schoolteacher, but *really* smart, like a genius."

I didn't have much trust in Pete's ability to tell a genius from a nutball. One thing I did trust, however, was my gut when it came to the Messams, and my gut was telling me that even if the twins *did* steal Uncle Dean's generator, it might be best just to let them have it. I said as much.

"That's the problem," Pete replied. "Everyone is so scared of the twins that they can get away with whatever they want to. And their dad is just as bad, maybe even worse. This is our chance to teach them a lesson. To show them once and for all that we're not going to take it anymore."

I shook my head. I could hardly believe what I was hearing. "They'd kill us!" I said.

"Only if we get caught," Pete replied, talking now as if the plan were already a go and we just had to work out a few small details, like how to stay alive and out of the hospital.

"We'll just have to be quiet and fast," he went on. "Like ninjas."

"Ninjas carrying a generator," I reminded him. "And that's if we even *could* carry it. Those things aren't exactly light, you know."

"It'll be fine," he assured me. "We'll take the little red wagon with us. It's still in the garage."

"The wagon?" I said doubtfully. "No way, it's too small." As far as I knew, it had never carried anything heavier than the twenty pounds of flyers that Pete and I used to deliver every Saturday morning.

"It'll work," Pete insisted. "I'll pull and you can push."

"I'm not pushing anything," I told him. As far as I was concerned, the whole idea was nuts.

Pete just stared at me for a moment. "So you're going to make me go on my own?"

"I'm not making you do anything," I said. "There's no point in you going either, not by yourself. You won't be able to get it without me."

"I could see if it was there at least," he said. "And if it is, then maybe I could make an anonymous tip to Constable Sheery."

"Don't be stupid," I said.

He shrugged, then hefted the ax again and reset the

log on the cutting block. "Never mind," he told me. "It's fine. Stay home if you want to. It's not like I really believed that you'd come anyway."

"What's that supposed to mean?"

He raised the ax and brought it down hard, splitting the log clean through the middle. "I just knew you'd be too scared is all."

"Don't be like that," I said, crossing my arms.

"Like what?" he asked, all innocent.

"You know what."

He shrugged again. "I'm just saying, somebody needs to do something."

We stared at each other for a second, him with his ax and his sweaty forehead, me with my arms crossed in front of me.

"If I come," I finally said, "then you have to promise me that we'll just look. That means no wagon. We'll take our bikes instead, and if the generator *is* there, we'll do like you said before and give Constable Sheery an anonymous tip."

Pete wasn't exactly used to letting me have my way, so he hesitated for a second before agreeing.

"All right," he said, "we'll just look around."

"Promise?"

He nodded. "I promise."

"Pinky swear?" I asked him.

He pinky swore.

"When?" I asked him, hoping he'd say tomorrow or maybe the next day, time enough for something to change his mind.

Instead, he said, "Tonight, after everyone is sleeping. We'll sneak out. Just be ready."

He handed me the ax and then went inside, leaving me to wonder what I had just gotten myself into.

FIFTEEN

As much as I loved birds, there was one that I actually used to have recurring nightmares about. The bird was a loggerhead shrike, and in my dream it stood nine feet tall instead of nine inches, its hooked bill like some Dark Age tool wrought from the blackest iron, meant for carving flesh.

Pete was always in the dream with me, both of us hanging in a jungle of giant thorns by the collars of our shirts, the air thick with heavy white fog. The thorns all around us were slick with blood, and flies the size of footballs buzzed past our heads.

The shrike was never there at first, so the dream always started the same, with a moment of pure confusion about where I was and how I'd gotten there. I'd reach back to feel the thorn through my shirt, and then turn my head sideways to find Pete beside me, not thrashing in the hopes of escape, as I always expected he would be, but simply hanging there like a wet towel, with tears running down from his eyes, knowing, it seemed, that there wasn't any point in struggling or screaming. That the two of us were doomed no matter what.

"Pete!" I'd yell at him. "Pete!" And then he'd look up at me with an expression of absolute hopelessness, while the shrike would pass overhead, its shadow just barely visible through the haze. A moment would go by, and then the shadow would appear again, this time settling right above us as the bird came to perch.

I'd hold my breath in the hopes that it might not hear me, that it might not realize I was there, but then it would occur to me that the bird must already know, and that the reason we were hanging on thorns was because it put us there, for a later meal. I'd feel myself shaking, my heart pounding, and then the hooked bill would suddenly slice down through the fog, the bird's masked eyes looking first at Pete and then at me, the motion almost reptilian in its jerkiness. It wasn't just looking, but trying to decide who to eat first. Thankfully, I always woke up before it made its choice.

This was no thanks to Pete, though, who was usually already awake and looking over at me from his own bed, my nightmare groans and my thrashing under my covers having stirred him from his own dreams, which were probably about scoring overtime goals or reeling in trophy-sized northern pike.

I'd sit up in my bed with my heart still banging, awash in residual terror but also relief. Embarrassment and anger would quickly follow. I couldn't understand why Pete never woke me up, why he always just watched and waited. I figured it was maybe spite, that he was letting me suffer in order to get back at me for interrupting his own sleep. Eventually I asked him.

"I figure if you get to the end of the dream, then maybe you'll stop having it," he told me simply. This was before he understood what the dream even was. I hadn't told him for fear that he'd laugh at me, which he did when I finally shared.

“A bird?!” he said, totally mystified. “*That’s* what you’ve been having nightmares about?”

“A giant bird!” I tried to explain. “One that impales things!”

He was obviously having trouble getting past the image of a twittering songbird, the kind that might fill a Disney-inspired forest with cheerful warbles from an open perch, with not a single shrike-like predator to be seen. Even after I told him about how shrikes truly *did* impale things, he still shook his head and laughed, as if it only got funnier the more I talked about it.

“I knew I shouldn’t have told you,” I finally said, but in the end I was glad that I did, not only because it felt good to get it off my chest, but because of something Pete asked me two days later.

“I don’t get it,” he said, pretty much out of the blue. “Why would a bird impale things? I mean, what’s the point?”

I didn’t know, which made me feel a little bit silly. Here I was having recurring nightmares about a bird that I hardly understood anything about.

The truth was, I’d made a point of *not* learning about the shrike. All I knew was that they often impaled their prey on thorns and barbed-wire fences, and that their Latin name meant "butcher bird." The only photo I'd ever seen of one was on page 91 in Mom's field identification guide, a photo that showed not only the bird—black and white and gray with a distinctive bandit mask—but also a cute little mouse, just hanging there, impaled through its tiny neck. The mouse's eyes were open and moist, and even in that tiny picture, which probably measured no more than two inches by two inches, it seemed as if light still shone there, as if the poor rodent were still alive.

The picture reminded me of Vlad the Impaler, and the story of how he'd once taken his evening meal while out on the grounds of his fifteenth-century castle, surrounded by the skewered bodies of hundreds of enemies whom he had impaled on the sharpened trunks of sawed-off trees. He'd wanted to look at them and listen to their screaming while he ate.

It was hard to believe that such a terrible story could actually be true, but according to my history teacher, Mr. Donner, it was. He taught us about it in class and finished the lesson by saying that Vlad the Impaler might have been the purest embodiment of cruelty that there ever was. I couldn't help but agree with him, which I think was why the picture of the shrike and the mouse bothered me so much. It almost seemed like photographic proof that birds could be just as bad as we were, never mind that this didn't fit with what I already understood about birds, how everything they did was out of economy, their every action a careful measure of energy gained versus energy spent.

But maybe I hadn't given shrikes a fair shot, and had taken their "butcher bird" reputation a little too literally. Clearly there had to be a purpose behind their morbid behavior. I just didn't know what that purpose was. So I went to the library to do some research.

I could've just stayed home and asked Mom, but I felt like this was something I had to learn on my own. Like it was important in a way that went beyond the simple absorption of ornithological facts.

Shrikes, I discovered, had been unjustly vilified. The reason they impaled their prey could not have been simpler or any more innocent. It had to do with the talons on their feet. They weren't designed like the talons found on larger birds of prey, so they weren't particularly well suited for holding and gripping the things that they killed. This made it harder for shrikes to tear away edible pieces with their sharp bills. Impaling was just their way of overcoming this disadvantage. It was kind of like a human using a fork to pin down a pork chop for his knife.

I continued reading, and discovered that small rodents and songbirds actually made up only a fraction of a typical shrike's diet. Mostly they just fed on insects, which didn't require any impaling at all. They simply caught them and ate them, like thousands of other birds all around the world, including the plain old house sparrows that lived in our backyard.

The more I learned, the more foolish I felt, and by the time I slid the books back into place on the alphabetized shelves, I had not only overcome any fear that I'd once had of the bandit-masked birds, but had also developed a newfound respect for them. Shrikes, I supposed, were sort of like the ghosts in a lot of horror movies. As soon as you understood who they actually were and what their reasons were for haunting in the first place, you couldn't help but sympathize with them.

I never had a shrike nightmare again. That ghost had moved on into the light, leaving me to wonder what other frightening things in life might be made less so with a little knowledge and understanding. I'd reconsidered the Messam twins, thinking how growing up with a violent father might have forced them down a path they could've otherwise avoided.

I'd decided that the next time they zeroed in on me for a knuckle sandwich or an atomic wedgie, I would try to talk to them instead of running.

Less than a week before my eleventh birthday, I got my chance.

"Just wait!" I said as they cornered me in the boot room at school. "You don't have to do this. Just because your dad is mean and angry all the time doesn't mean you guys have to be, too. You can be better than that." It came out precisely as I had rehearsed it, but the next part didn't exactly go as planned.

The twins stared at me as if pink and purple polka dots had just broken out all over my skin. Then they casually picked me up, flipped me upside down, and stuffed me into the nearest garbage can. With only my legs sticking out of the can, they tipped it onto its side and proceeded to roll me all the way across the playground and down the alley behind the school, occasionally kicking the garbage can and laughing all the way.

I was so dizzy afterward that I couldn't stand up for a full five minutes. I felt like a kernel of corn that had gone through the popper. I guess it taught me an important lesson, though: The cruelty of birds might be an illusion, but the kind that lives in the hearts of boys like Lester and Lars is very real indeed, no matter its true root cause.

SIXTEEN

"Just be ready," Pete had told me, but of course I wasn't. I'd had too many hours to consider what might go wrong, what probably *would* go wrong. I couldn't believe that I'd ever agreed to the plan in the first place. I wondered if Pete was having second thoughts as well.

"Sneak downstairs and get us our shoes," he whispered to me in the darkness, which pretty much answered my question. "I'll get the window open."

It was past midnight now, and we finally had the "all clear" sound that we'd been waiting for: Dad snoring from across the hall.

I shifted in the darkness. “Maybe this isn’t such a good idea,” I said.

Pete rounded on me. “No way!” he said. “You can’t back out now!”

“I’m not backing out,” I told him. “I was just thinking—”

“Oh yeah? Well, don’t. Just go and get us our shoes. And stay off the creaky stairs. You know which ones they are.”

I did know, and since Pete had just brought it up, I could no longer purposely step on them in order to sabotage the plan. My only hope now was that our old sliding window might jam up inside its frame. It did that sometimes, although it was usually only right after it rained.

I managed the stairs without any problems and was back in our room in under a minute. Pete, meanwhile, had made short work of the window.

I took a deep breath and tried to steel myself.

“Here,” said Pete. “Put this on.”

He handed me a ninja mask—the same one I’d worn the Halloween before last. Pete had one, too, as well as a pair of nunchucks stuck in his belt. I almost asked him where my weapon was, but since I couldn't imagine actually using one (against a Messam or anyone else), I held my tongue.

"Just try not to fall on your head," Pete said. And then he was up and over the sill, and into the leafy arms of the elm tree beyond. He moved as if inspired by the mask he wore, swinging and dropping from one branch to the next, even flipping himself upside down at one point, just to show off.

My own journey down was much more methodical. I moved less like a ninja and more like a three-toed sloth on a vine. By the time my feet touched grass, Pete had already gone into the garage and come back out again. Not with our bikes, but with the wagon. He also had a can of WD-40, to grease the wheels to keep them from squeaking.

"What are you doing?" I asked him. "You promised!"

He shrugged. "I changed my mind."

"You pinky swore!"

"Just think about it for a second," he tried to reason with me. "It doesn't make sense to take our bikes. I mean, what if the generator is right outside? Just sitting there in the yard? We might as well take it while we can."

I felt like slugging him. "And what's Dad going to say?" I asked him. "When we tell him where it was and how we got it?"

"We won't tell him," Pete said simply. "We'll just put it in the back of Uncle Dean's truck when we get back, with a note on it. It'll look like someone dropped it off in the night, because of a guilty conscience or something."

He reached into his pocket and took out a piece of paper, unfolding it so I could read it.

I believe this belongs to you was all it said, in bold black marker. Pete had obviously been thinking ahead, which meant that he'd changed his mind long before we climbed out our window.

I took off my mask and threw it on the ground, so angry now that I could feel heat in both of my cheeks.

"I'm going back," I told him.

"Why?" said Pete. "We're already both outside. We might as well just go."

"You should've told me!" I blurted, no longer caring if anyone heard me.

"Shh! Don't yell! I was *going* to tell you, but then I decided that it would be better if I didn't."

"Better for who?" I said.

"Everyone," he replied. "If we come back with the generator."

I just stared at him. "You *pinky swore*," I said again. The pinky swear was supposed to be sacred.

"I meant it when I said it," he tried to reassure me. "I just changed my mind."

I looked down at the little red wagon and was reminded of the last time that Pete and I had taken it out, how we'd dumped our flyers that day instead of delivering them—and not for the first time. Pete had talked me into it. He said that nobody actually wanted them anyway and that nobody would notice or complain. He was wrong, of course. Dad turned red when he found out. I honestly believed that smoke might pour out of his ears.

"What's the big deal?" Pete had asked, ignoring the lit fuse and showing no sign of remorse at all. "They're just flyers. Everybody throws them in the garbage anyway."

"And if they do," Dad replied evenly, "that's *their* choice to make, not yours. What exactly do you think you're getting paid for? To push a wagon twelve feet and lift the lid on a garbage can? And then what? Go to the park and play around on the monkey bars? What's going to happen when you're older? Do you honestly think that someone will pay you for doing nothing? That you'll be able to just stand around all day and then collect a check? Is that how you think the world works?" He looked from Pete to me and then back to Pete again. "Well, is it?"

"No," we both replied meekly.

"Well, you could have fooled me," Dad went on. "How many times did you dump them? Once? Twice?"

"Three times," I admitted.

"And where's the money you earned from those three batches?" Dad asked.

"We spent it," Pete replied. On hockey cards and sour candies.

"That's what I thought," said Dad. "So you can pay Mr. Young back with labor. You're going to take turns cutting his lawn for the rest of the summer. Backyard and front."

Mr. Young was the man who gave us the job.

"The rest of the summer?!" screamed Pete. "But that's not fair!"

"Keep it up and you'll be shoveling his walk all winter, too," Dad warned him.

Pete opened his mouth and then closed it again. He stared at Dad for a moment before storming off to his room. I kept standing right where I was, waiting to be dismissed and feeling smaller than I had ever felt before. I felt angry, too, both at Pete for talking me into dumping the flyers in the first place and at myself for letting it happen two more times.

"Well?" Dad asked me. "What do you have to say for yourself?"

All I could muster was a simple "I'm sorry."

Dad nodded and sighed. "I hope you are, Ben. I really do. I expected more from you."

Of all the things he could have said, of course he had to say that. I felt skewered by my shame.

"Go to your room," he told me, somewhat more gently now, as if he sensed how much he'd just hurt me. "And don't come out again until I say so."

It was impossible to look at the wagon without thinking of that afternoon. Or at least for me it was; I wasn't so sure about Pete. He never did seem particularly bothered by what we'd done, only that we'd gotten caught for it.

"Well?" he asked me. "Are you going to come with me or not? I need your help."

His tone was almost pleading now. He clearly didn't want to go alone.

I stood there a moment longer before bending down to pick up my ninja mask. Pete had never taken his off. How strange he looked in the pale light of the moon, a hopeful shadow warrior with his little red wagon, its wheels and axles freshly greased.

We left without another word, out through the gate and into the dark of the night.

SEVENTEEN

The Messam house sat at the very end of Warman Street, right up against the berm that ran alongside the railroad tracks. Pete and I approached from the alley, our little wagon temporarily parked in a patch of weeds beside a garbage can.

The back fence was leaning in some places and completely fallen in others, the old white paint on the weathered pickets faded and peeling like dry dead skin. The gate itself was nowhere to be seen, as if someone had come along and stolen it just for the lumber. A four-foot gap marked where it had stood. Pete paused before crossing this threshold.

"Stay behind me," he whispered through his ninja mask, as if I had any intention at all of rushing past him into the grass, which the Messams obviously never bothered to mow. It was higher than our knees. The lights were all off in the house, the windows dark.

"Maybe I should just stand watch," I replied, my heart pounding at the thought of the twins gazing out at us from between their curtains. I strained my eyes to find a reflection through the uppermost windows, a glint from an eye in the darkness behind the glass. But there was nothing.

"Don't be a wuss," Pete said quietly. "Just stay low and don't make any noise. They're probably not even home."

I was willing to bet that their dad would be, though. I just had to hope that he'd be drunk and passed out by this time of night.

I wondered if those Desert Storm stories were true, and if what I was feeling now, as I waded into the long grass with shaking hands and wobbly knees, was anything like what soldiers might feel when plunging headlong into enemy territory. At least Sergeant Messam would have had a rifle. All I had was Pete and his pair of cheap red nunchucks, which I knew for a fact he'd never really learned how to use. If it came down to it, he was probably just as likely to knock himself out as he was either one of the twins.

I paused for a second and wondered what the heck we were doing here, how I'd let him talk me into this.

"C'mon," he whispered back to me over his shoulder. "Quit screwing around."

I wasn't screwing around, though; I was scared. I felt like I'd somehow stranded myself in the middle of an active minefield. My best chance now was to turn around and retrace my steps back to safety, only I couldn't because Pete was counting on me.

"Hurry up!" he said, his voice slightly more than a whisper now. He was crouched so low in the grass that I could barely even see him.

I took a deep breath and continued on.

Pete took his nunchucks out from his belt and headed off toward the garage.

"Watch your step," he told me a moment later, as if land mines were now on his mind as well, which of course they weren't. He was simply warning me about the numerous empty glass pop bottles that were strewn about in an old sandbox-turned-firepit at the edge of the yard.

I looked down at the bottles and remembered Uncle Dean saying that whoever had broken into his shop had busted into the pop machine as well. I shook my head. We'd been right in our suspicions, it seemed. Not that I'd had much doubt.

I placed my feet with care, my gaze moving away from the bottles to the firepit itself. In the center of the ash pile was a hollow spot, as if the ashes had been cleared away in order to find something, perhaps the charred remains of something they'd burned. I leaned in closer and, sure enough, something was there, something that I couldn't quite identify on account of it having been blackened by the fire. I don't know why, but I picked it up, my fingers falling into natural finger-holes that, upon closer inspection—and to my horror—I realized were actually eye sockets, empty above a small nasal cavity and jaws with sharp little teeth. I was holding the skull of a cat.

I dropped it, my breath hitching as I took a step back. My foot came down on one of the bottles, which rolled beneath me and sent me flying. I landed hard on my back, the impact forcing most of the air from my lungs. I sat up, hurt and wheezing.

Pete spun around. "Darn it, Ben!" he whispered. "I told you to watch your step!"

It was obvious that he hadn't seen what I had, the evidence of a teenage sacrifice in the form of a skull. There were two sticks as well, just off to the side, both of them sharpened to fine points. Good for poking.

I'd seen enough. I no longer cared if the twins had the generator. They could keep it. The only thing that mattered to me now was getting the heck out of there, away from those two empty eye sockets, staring up from the ash and the sand.

I got up and ran, back through the overgrown grass and out through the space in the ramshackle fence, adrenaline fueling my muscles and narrowing my mind, neutralizing every thought that wasn't connected to the word *escape*.

I guess I just assumed that Pete would follow, or maybe I didn't even consider him at all. All I knew for sure was that I reached the end of the alley in the blink of an eye, and that when I got there, my brother wasn't behind me.

I stopped for a moment and waited, my heart pounding, ears ringing as if they'd been boxed. *One Mississippi, two Mississippi, three*... Still no Pete. Now what?

And then I heard it: the unmistakable sound of Messam laughter, coming from down the street. I turned my head to see the twins about a hundred feet away on their BMX bikes, below a stop sign that Lester appeared to be vandalizing.

Despite their being identical, it was easy to tell the twins apart. Lester always wore a baseball cap (the camouflage kind that hunters liked) and Lars never did. Lester usually wore it backward, but not always. Tonight he had it on straight. He was wearing a black pullover and black gloves as well—they both were—and was holding a can of spray paint. I heard the loose marble sound as he shook it, and then the hiss as he set about spraying. Laughter again.

I was standing out in the open. All they had to do was turn their heads and they would see me. Heck, I was probably *already* visible in their periphery, which was exactly why I hadn't moved yet. If there's one thing that birding teaches you, it's that motion is often the surest way of attracting attention. Sometimes if you just stand perfectly still, nature will go on about its business right around you. Birds will sing and forage as if you're not there; squirrels will come out to investigate their surroundings; if you're lucky, you might even get a fox or a coyote to cross your path.

The twins began to move off, but not before horsing around a little on their bikes, the light from the nearest streetlamp reflecting off their spokes and rims as they attempted a series of freestyle tricks, all of which I'd seen before.

The twins liked to show off on their bikes in front of the school, doing tail-whips and bar-spins as the school bus honked at them to get out of the way. Some of the tricks looked borderline suicidal (one of them was even called a "suicide no hand") and they didn't always go as planned either. As good as the twins were, it was almost inevitable that one of them would slip off a foot-peg or mistime a jump, resulting in a wipeout. The smart kids knew better than to laugh when that happened, but it seemed that there was always at least one numbskull who couldn't resist a quick little chuckle or a serves-you-right smile. A lucky few got away with it, but more often than not, the twins would close the curtain on their bike show and then wipe the floor with whoever the poor sap was who just couldn't keep it together.

I was guilty of laughing once myself, but thankfully Pete was there to elbow me in the side before anyone noticed. If there was one thing I could always count on my older brother for, it was that: protecting me—even if I didn't want it or thought I didn't need it. He definitely wouldn't have left *me* alone in the Messams' backyard.

Not that the twins were actually in their yard, of course, although they might be in a moment. It all depended on whether or not they turned right or just kept going straight. I silently willed them to pedal off down the block, only to feel my heart sink as Lester said, "C'mon," and then aimed his handlebars toward the road home.

I hesitated a second longer, praying that Pete would suddenly appear from the darkness, but he didn't, which meant that I had to move, and quickly. My adrenaline was ebbing, though, my body feeling three times heavier than it had only minutes before. Nevertheless, I ran, the night feeling suddenly thick and substantial around me, like something that might harden if I stopped.

I saw a light as I approached the fence, from Pete's little flashlight, I realized. He was shining it through the window of the Messams' garage, and had his face almost right up against the glass, completely oblivious to the fact that the twins were probably coming up the front driveway at that very second.

"Psstt!" I whispered, as loud as I dared to. "Twins at nine o'clock!"

Pete glanced my way first and then in the direction indicated, his head jerking with fresh alertness, as if my warning had been immediately followed by the sound of bikes being dropped to the pavement in the driveway out front.

His flashlight winked out a second later, at exactly the same moment that a voice cut through the darkness.

"Hey! What the hell do you think you're doing?"

I knew that Pete was fast—definitely faster than I

was—but I didn't realize just how fast until that moment. He shot toward me as if he had a jetpack strapped to his back, his feet barely touching the ground.

Lester appeared a split second later, not on his bike now but sprinting, his arms pumping madly. I only saw him for an instant, but it was all the time I needed to know that I was doomed, that Pete would overtake me easily and that Lester would catch me before I even got out of the alley. My only hope was to hide, and pray that Lester had only seen one of us. Pete might be able to outrun him on his own, but not if he had to wait for his slow little brother.

I took a few quick steps and dove sideways into a big patch of rhubarb growing along the fence. I curled myself into a ball and tried to be still, listening for the sound of Lester's footsteps. What I heard instead, though, was a loud and metallic *snap* sound, followed by the sort of scream that, up until that moment, I'd only ever heard in horror flicks. It was shrill and strangled and desperate, and it kept on going.

An icy chill ran through me as I lay there on the ground, wondering what the heck had just happened, and completely unaware that Pete had slid to a stop as soon as he realized I was no longer with him. I jumped as he grabbed my arm and tried to pull me up.

"Shh!" he whispered, as if anyone would hear the sound of rustling rhubarb leaves over the ear-splitting wail that was coming from the Messams' backyard.

"Get it open! Get it open!" Lester now screamed. It hardly sounded like Lester at all, though. It barely sounded human.

Get what *open?* I wondered as Pete pulled me again. I went with him this time, jogging at first and then running again, despite the fact that I could tell Lester was in no shape to follow.

A full block away and we could still hear him, whimpering, almost painfully pleading. We stopped for a minute.

"He's injured," I said stupidly. "Bad, I think."

"No crap, Sherlock," Pete replied. "Why did you stop?"

"I thought maybe you could outrun him on your own," I told him.

"And leave you there?" he asked me.

I shrugged. "I left you."

"Yeah, well, you came back."

"What happened?" I asked. "What was that sound?"

Pete shook his head. "I don't know," he said. "We should get home, though."

I reached up to take off my ninja mask, but Pete told me to leave it on for now, just in case anyone saw us.

"We left the wagon," I said.

"Forget it," he told me. "We'll have to get it later."

"What about the generator?" I asked him. "Did you see it? Was it in the garage?"

He shook his head. "I didn't see anything."

EIGHTEEN

I was still so shaken up by the time we got home that I couldn't even climb the tree back up to our open window. I tried, but my arms had all the strength of a pair of pipe cleaners. My legs were no better.

"You've climbed it a hundred times!" Pete said impatiently.

Couldn't he see how bad I was shaking? I felt like I might throw up and pulled off my ninja mask just in case. It had been making me feel claustrophobic anyway, like a mummy wrapped up way too tight.

"You go," I told him. I hadn't even gotten my breath

back yet from all the running. "You can sneak down and open the back door for me."

"Are you crazy?" he said. "Do you *want* us to get caught?"

I shook my head. "I can't climb it," I said. "Not right now." I could barely even stand up. "Maybe if we just wait a few minutes..." I leaned back to steady myself against the tree trunk. My back still hurt from my fall by the twins' firepit, but it was my brain that had suffered the worst of the bruising. I kept seeing that blackened cat skull, kept hearing the awful sound of Lester screaming, as if he himself were being burned alive in some hellish firepit.

"Dad's a first responder," Pete reminded me. "He might get called. Heck, he might've gotten called already."

"Crap," I said. I probably should have thought of that, but I hadn't.

"Here, I'll give you a boost," said Pete. He went down on one knee and cupped his hands together.

I took a deep breath and tried to will strength to my jellied limbs. Pete was right; I'd climbed it a hundred times.

I stepped onto his makeshift platform expecting a

gentle lift up to the branch that I otherwise would have needed to jump to reach, but instead he tried to launch me, taking me by surprise. My knee buckled at the sudden jerk, throwing me off balance. I windmilled my arms in desperation, but all I found was air.

Pete swore, his cupped hands coming apart as the two of us collapsed to the ground in a pile.

"You're hopeless," he said a second later. "Just wait by the back door."

And with that, he scurried up the tree like a squirrel on a mission, disappearing through our window before I'd even managed to get back to my feet. I hobbled over to the door and waited. A few seconds passed, and then a few seconds more. A full minute went by. I began to worry. Was Pete just messing with me, or had something happened?

I was just on the verge on convincing myself he'd been caught when the knob began to turn. I started to let out a sigh of relief, only to realize that it wasn't Pete on the other side of the door.

"Ben?" said my uncle Dean, looking out at me with obvious surprise. He had an unlit cigar sticking out from the corner of his mouth. Pete stood behind him, wearing pajamas now rather than clothes. He must have quickly changed before coming downstairs, most likely just in case Mom or Dad saw him outside of our room. He could have lied about why he was up.

"What on earth are you doing outside at one in the morning?" Uncle Dean asked.

Lying wasn't something that had ever come particularly naturally to me, and neither did thinking on my feet. I was more of a brooder, long on thinking and late on action. I averted my gaze to the ninja mask still in my hand, as if the guise of the shadow warrior might somehow inspire me instead of just incriminating me further. Uncle Dean waited a moment for me to say something before finally turning to look back at Pete.

"Just got up for a glass of water, huh?" he said.

That must have been what Pete had told him. Uncle Dean had probably even believed it. Unfortunately for us, though, Uncle Dean had already made up his mind to go outside and smoke a cigar. It was just bad luck and stupid coincidence that when he opened the door, he found me standing there.

"Well, I *was* going to get some water," Pete replied, "so technically I wasn't lying."

Pete can be a real dope sometimes.

"It was just a dumb dare," I said as the ponderous gears in my brain finally clicked and engaged. "Pete called me a chicken. He said if I wasn't scared of turning to glass, then I wouldn't mind standing outside in the dark for ten whole minutes to prove it."

Uncle Dean looked skeptical. "What's the mask for?" he asked me.

I shrugged. "Ninjas aren't scared of anything."

"He was supposed to come in through the window," Pete added. "But he's a numbnuts. He fell and hurt himself, so I had to come down and let him back in."

"You all right?" Uncle Dean asked me.

"It's my back," I said. "I landed funny." The fact that I actually *was* in pain probably helped me sell my story.

Uncle Dean shook his head at us. "You turkeys should know better," he said. "You're not eight and nine anymore. What if you'd fallen harder and had to go to the hospital? Your mom and dad have enough to worry about already."

"I know," I said. "I'm sorry."

"Me too," Pete agreed. "It was stupid. You're not going to tell Dad, are you?"

Uncle Dean sighed. "I suppose not. But only on the condition that you both walk the straight and narrow from here on out. Capiche?"

"Capiche," we agreed in unison.

"Good," said Uncle Dean. "Now, get to bed before I change my mind."

We went, both of us treading as quietly as we could. It was clear now that Dad's CB radio must have stayed quiet. Maybe it wasn't his turn in the first responder rotation, or maybe Constable Sheery had simply decided that where the Messam family was concerned, it might be best to send someone who carried a pistol and a badge; whatever the case, I was grateful to fall into my bed without having to answer any more questions.

"I bet it was an animal trap," said Pete after a moment of quiet. "Set up in the grass. Lester probably forgot about it when he saw me and then accidentally set it off."

The idea hadn't even occurred to me. It made sense, and definitely explained what that loud *snap* sound had been before Lester started screaming. It also explained why he'd been yelling "get it open."

"God," I said. "We could've stepped on it." The realization sent a cold shiver up my back.

"Yup," Pete agreed, "we could've. If you think about it, it's actually a *good* thing we snuck out. Thanks to us, that trap is no longer a danger to anyone else."

"Yeah, I guess," I said. Better Lester than another innocent animal, I supposed. Maybe there was such a thing as karma after all.

NINETEEN

The trap belonged to James Messam, who hunted sometimes. It was one of those big metal ones with interlocking teeth. The twins had apparently set it up without their father's knowledge or permission—to catch a coyote, they told Constable Sheery. A rabid one that Lars claimed had tried to attack him the night before.

"Rabid coyote, my butt," said Pete.

"More like another stray cat," I added.

Constable Sheery had come by in the morning to

have coffee with Dad—as he sometimes did—and had filled him in on everything that had happened, mentioning along the way that the twins had chased off a "burglar in a ski mask."

Pete and I had been eavesdropping from the top of the stairwell. We both breathed a sigh of relief that only one of us had been seen, and that the ninja mask had been misidentified. It meant that the twins wouldn't know who to take revenge on—not that Lester was going to be taking revenge on anyone anytime soon. Constable Sheery said that his leg was mangled so bad that they had to transport him to Paulson, where he'd probably be staying awhile to recover from emergency surgery.

"One twin down and one to go," Pete joked.

"Maybe we'll get lucky and Lars will turn to glass," I said.

"Doubt it," Pete replied. "Most likely Lester will just get better and then come back meaner than he was before."

"Probably," I agreed, although it was hard to imagine what meaner would even look like when it came to the twins.

Constable Sheery talked to Dad about the glass plague as well, saying that there was a phone number people could call now if they lost somebody. The government was compiling a database and trying to work out some sort of system for emotional and financial aid.

"It's chaos," Constable Sheery said. "Absolute chaos."

"If there's anything I can do..." said Dad.

"I'll let you know. In the meantime, you just worry about looking after your boys. Have you sat them down yet? To go over the ifs and maybes?"

"Not yet," Dad admitted.

"Well, I wouldn't put it off for too much longer if I were you. We've been lucky here in Griever's Mill. Paulson, too. A lot of other places have been hit repeatedly, and they say that the numbers are always higher each time. Chicago lost sixty in the first blackout, then ninety, then three hundred."

"Bloody heck," said Dad.

"Yes, sirree," Constable Sheery agreed. "I hope our good pastor is preparing himself. Could soon be a lot of folks in sudden need of services for the shattered."

"Let's hope not," Dad said gravely.

There was a moment of silence, and then the clink of a coffee cup being set on a saucer. "Anyway," Constable Sheery continued, "I guess I should probably make tracks."

We heard him get up from the dining room table, and so we crept back into our room before he could pass by the stairwell and see us. We kept listening, though, from just inside our door.

"Where's that brother of yours this morning?" Constable Sheery asked. He was in the front entryway now.

"Not entirely sure," Dad told him. "He said he had to see a man about a horse."

"Hmm, not literally, I suppose. Might not be a bad idea, mind you. I doubt we'll be seeing many fuel tankers rolling through in the next little while. Speaking of which, how much gas you got in that truck of yours?"

"Almost full," Dad replied.

"Good," said Constable Sheery. "Keep it that way if you can. Waste not, want not, as they say."

Dad said that wouldn't be a problem since he wasn't

going to be working for the next three weeks anyway. "Booked it off months ago," he added. "Who knew?"

"Some vacation, eh?"

"Some vacation," Dad agreed.

Pete and I watched from the window as Constable Sheery got in his cruiser and drove off. Dad was at our door a few minutes later, asking if he could come in.

"Sure," I answered as Pete sat down on the edge of his bed and picked up an Uncanny X-Men comic, as if he'd spent the last little while just reading.

Dad looked down at him as he came in, his eyes narrowed skeptically.

"Constable Sheery thinks that I need to have a talk with you boys," he told us. "But since you were listening in, I guess you already knew that."

Pete tried his best to put on an innocent face, but Dad wasn't buying it.

"I wasn't born yesterday," he said, his hands on his hips now.

"Fine," said Pete, "but we didn't hear *everything*." As if eavesdropping had degrees of severity and hearing only part of a conversation was sort of like *almost* committing a crime.

"I'm sure," said Dad. "He was right, though. I've been putting it off, and I shouldn't. It's too important."

"It's okay," said Pete. "I already know what you're going to say."

Dad raised an eyebrow. "Is that a fact?"

Pete nodded. "You're going to say that if something happens, we'll have to stay strong and look out for each other, and that we'll have to stop acting like kids and start acting like grown-ups. Like men."

"You think you could handle that?" asked Dad, crossing his arms in front of him. "Because it's one thing to say something, and another to actually follow through on it. Nothing comes easy. Not in this world, and probably not in the next one either. You boys need to understand that."

"I understand," said Pete.

"Do you?" Dad asked him.

Pete nodded. I nodded, too, even though I really wasn't sure. How could I be? Dad was talking about being an adult and I was still a million miles away from that. So was Pete, no matter what he might like to believe.

"Good," said Dad. "But I don't think we need to start worrying about any of that yet. You guys have me and your mother both, as well as your uncle Dean. I think the odds of you ending up on your own are pretty slim."

"But it's possible," I said.

Dad looked at me like he wanted to say it wasn't, but he couldn't. That wouldn't be honest, and if there was one thing that Dad valued above pretty much everything else, it was honesty. That, and hard work.

"It's possible," he admitted. "But if worse comes to worst, you can always call Constable Sheery, or go to Pastor Nolan. Okay?"

We nodded.

"Where's Mom?" I asked. It wasn't like her to not be around if there was a guest at our house, and the whole time Pete and I had been eavesdropping, I hadn't heard her voice even once. Normally, she'd have been in and out of the kitchen, offering Constable Sheery cookies or cake or just a refill on his coffee.

"In the backyard with her binoculars and her notepad," said Dad. "She's having a count day."

"A count day?" I asked. "But she never said anything to me...."

A count day was one where you spent as much time as you could at one location and counted all the different species that came along. It was something that birders everywhere did a few times each year—mostly during migration, though, not in the middle of summer. I usually helped Mom whenever she did one. It was something that I looked forward to.

"She wasn't planning on doing one," Dad explained. "It was my idea. I thought it might put her at ease."

"She still could've told me," I said.

"Next time," Dad replied.

I snuck a look at Mom's notepad a little while later, after she came back inside, and noticed something strange. She'd only written down the names of three birds, and there were only seven checkmarks in total. Usually I could have gotten that many by just listening from inside the house with a window open. Mom must have seen more birds than that. It didn't make sense, unless she'd started the count and then quit just a short way into it, which maybe she did. The whole point of a bird count was to gather information that could later be passed on to ornithologists for their studies, but with the world going to crap all over, I doubted that bird studies were going to be very high on anyone's priority list. Why bother keeping tabs on avian populations when our own was plummeting faster than a peregrine in a stoop?

TWENTY

When Uncle Dean got back from wherever it was that he'd gone, he had something large and square shaped in the box of his truck. It had a fat wire harness sticking out of it.

Dad quirked an eyebrow at him when he came inside. "Went to see a man about a horse, eh?"

"Woman, actually," Uncle Dean replied. "And who needs horsepower when you've got solar!"

"Where on earth did you get a solar panel from?" Mom asked him, but then she held up a hand to stall his answer. "Wait," she said, "never mind. I know exactly where you got it from."

So did I, or at least I was pretty sure. There was a greenhouse that we always passed on the highway whenever we went to Turtle Lake (our usual camping and fishing spot), and on its roof were six big solar panels—the only ones I'd ever seen. The greenhouse belonged to a middle-aged widow named Mrs. O'Keefe. She brought her car in to Uncle Dean's garage all the time, always complaining of weird noises that no one else could ever hear.

I overheard Mom tell Dad once that there was nothing even wrong with the car and that Mrs. O'Keefe's behavior was "unseemly." I wasn't sure exactly what she meant. I just remember that Dad replied by saying, "She's just lonely, that's all."

"I made her a deal," Uncle Dean said. "I promised I'd bring it back to her before winter. She doesn't really need all six of them during the summertime anyway."

"And that's it?" said Dad. "She just let you show up and take it?"

"Not exactly," said Uncle Dean. "I also had to promise her something else first."

"What?" Dad asked him.

"Dinner and a movie, once all this craziness is over."

"Oh, Dean," said Mom. Dad just laughed and shook his head.

Pete was still looking out the window at the panel in the truck box. "Do you even know how to hook it up?" he asked.

Uncle Dean shrugged. "Well, I unhooked it. It's a beast, though. I'll definitely need a hand getting it up to the roof."

"I'll help!" offered Pete.

"You can help from the ground," Mom quickly replied.

Pete grumbled and rolled his eyes.

"I think the two of us can manage it," said Dad.

They did, too, although not until after Uncle Dean had eaten a sandwich, during which time Dad recounted pretty much everything that Constable Sheery had told him, including the part about the Messam twins chasing off a would-be burglar in a mask sometime after midnight.

Uncle Dean narrowed his eyes and then looked right at me, my heart suddenly doing double-time in my chest. The fact that I'd been outside with a ninja mask at the exact same time of the night Lester had gotten hurt obviously wasn't lost on him. The only question now was, would he tell Dad?

I sat there in agony as he slowly chewed and swallowed his last bite of peanut butter and jelly and washed it down with a big gulp of iced tea.

Here it comes, I thought. *I'm totally busted.* Pete would be, too. It didn't matter that Uncle Dean had actually only seen me outside. Dad would never believe that I had gone to the Messams' house all on my own. I wasn't the scaredy-cat that Pete liked to make me out to be, but I wasn't exactly SEAL Team Six material either. No, we were definitely both up the creek without a paddle.

Uncle Dean opened his mouth, but before he could say anything, Dad started talking.

"I think I've still got those straps that we used when we hauled that big old deep freeze to the dump," he said. "I should go dig them out. No sense in us wrecking our backs if we don't have to."

Uncle Dean considered this for a second, then replied, "Good idea. And while you're doing that, I'll get the boys to help me carry the bank of batteries." He looked our way. "Go on and get your shoes on, guys."

I could tell from the look in his eyes that it wasn't batteries he was thinking about. He just wanted to get us outside, where he could question us without Mom overhearing. As it happened, though, she followed us out. I guess she wanted to make sure that we didn't electrocute ourselves on the terminals.

There were only four batteries in total, so we each took one and carried it around the house to the backyard. I grabbed mine last, and Uncle Dean hung back for a second to say something to me.

"I don't know what you and your brother got up to last night," he said quietly, "but I know that you lied to me, and I expect a full explanation as soon as we're through installing this panel. It's either that, or I go to your dad. Your call."

I swallowed hard. "I'll tell you," I promised.

"Good," he said. "Now, get moving, and watch where you're holding that thing or you'll end up with grease all over your hands."

TWENTY-ONE

Slowly but surely, Dad and Uncle Dean managed to muscle the panel up the ladder and onto the roof, where it was apparently a whole lot hotter than down on the ground. Dad swore after kneeling down for just a second, the sun-roasted shingles singeing his bare knees.

"That's what you get for wearing cargo shorts," Uncle Dean told him.

I'd never seen Uncle Dean in anything other than blue jeans. I guess we were kind of alike in that way. I didn't ever wear shorts either, unless I was swimming.

Pete and I watched from the lawn in the front yard,

far enough away that if anything fell, it wouldn't land on us. Mom stood beside us.

A few of our neighbors came by for a minute or two, all of them wanting to know where the panel came from and whether there were any more of them available. Mr. Olson offered to lend a hand, but Dad politely declined, saying, "I think we've got a pretty good handle on things here, Steve. Thanks, though."

One of Mr. Olson's two young daughters, who couldn't have been older than four, looked up at her father and said, "Daddy, how come they're putting a giant mirror up on the roof?"

"It's a magic mirror," he told her. "It makes electricity."

"Oooohhhhh!" she said, to which her older sister replied, "You don't even know what electricity is."

"Do, too," the little girl insisted.

"C'mon, you two," Mr. Olson told them. "Let's go."

They continued arguing as they headed back down the sidewalk, numerous sections of which were decorated with the colored chalk that the girls often used to draw out squares for hopscotch. Mom smiled at them as they went, and I wondered if she ever felt sad that she only had sons.

"That takes care of the rails," Uncle Dean said from the roof. "Should be smooth sailing from here." He put down his drill and then stood the panel up on its side to reposition it, only to pause as Dad tapped him on the shoulder and directed his attention to the north. They both stood there staring in that direction for a moment, and then slowly turned their heads and their bodies all the way around, taking in the whole horizon.

"What is it?" Mom asked them. "What are you seeing?" She turned in a circle herself and stood on her tiptoes to no avail. Above us was only blue.

Dad and Uncle Dean just kept on staring.

"It can't possibly be moving that fast," said Dad. "Can it?"

Uncle Dean glanced quickly over his left shoulder, and then back again over his right, as if he were trapped in a room and the walls were closing in on him. He didn't need to answer Dad's question; the truth was written all over his face.

I still couldn't see any darkness from where I was standing, but I could feel it now, like a tightening noose encircling our town.

Mom put one hand on my shoulder and one on Pete's and told us to get inside.

"Finish it later!" she yelled up at Dad and Uncle Dean.

Pete and I only went as far as the front step, where we stopped to wait for everyone else.

"Look!" said Pete, pointing across the street, where a billowing blackness was already starting to encroach on the sky.

Mom yelled again, to which Dad replied, "We just need to secure it! It's a handful of screws. Won't take but a minute."

It was a minute they wouldn't get, though. There was a sudden thump from up on the roof, followed by the harsh *skkssshhhhh* sound of something sliding along rough shingles, and Dad saying, "No! No! No!" And then the solar panel came over the eaves, its wire harness trailing behind like a comet's tail. It hit the ground with the crash and crunch of broken glass and dented metal—details that I registered only vaguely, as my attention had shifted from one falling thing to another, the second being dark and human shaped, arms raised in a final pose that would last only seconds.

He landed fingers first on the sidewalk, so that his hands and his arms shattered a fraction of a second before his head and body, the fragments exploding out in every direction, peppering the nearest feeders like so much shrapnel, while his clothes came to rest in a strangely neat little pile, baseball cap first and running shoes last, both of them landing soles down and toes pointed in the same direction.

I might have flinched at the moment of impact, but other than that I don't think I moved. It had all just happened so fast, like some sleight-of-hand trick my brain couldn't keep up with.

I saw the pieces and heard Mom scream; I even felt a slight tingle on my left cheek where one of the fragments had grazed me in passing, but it wasn't until Dad stepped right to the edge of the roof and stood there looking down that I finally made the connection between the carnage and my uncle Dean. A sudden heaviness pulled at my insides. Tears welled up in my eyes.

"Dean?" said Dad, my heart breaking at his confusion, at the disbelief on his face. His younger brother had vanished instantly, like flash powder fed to a fire.

Mom begged Dad to get off the roof before the same thing happened to him. She was yelling at us as well, her fear as deep as the sky was black above us.

I felt a surge of fear then, too, not only for Dad but also for myself. The possibility of turning to glass was scary enough, but now I had to consider the timing of it. Like what if it happened to me while I was running or climbing a tree, or even just coming down the stairs in the morning for breakfast? The thought of it made me want to move in slow motion. I looked up at the sky again, and watched how it roiled and swirled, how it seemed to possess its own currents, a million shades of gray swimming this way and that. It would have been beautiful had it not been so terrifying, and as I stood there, marveling at it, I somehow knew that this time was different, that Griever's Mill was about to join the countless other places that had already experienced the full wrath of whatever force this was.

The ladder clattered as Dad climbed down the rungs. He paused at the bottom, his eyes wide with shock and grief as he surveyed the damage. There were bits of Uncle Dean everywhere, some of them having flown as far away as the driveway. Dad would collect them, I knew, every single one he could find, although what he would do with them after, I had no idea. I had a brief vision of him sitting on a stool in the garage, hunched over like some sort of tinker with a tube of model glue, valiantly trying to put Humpty Dumpty back together again.

He finally turned to look at Pete and me. "Are you two deaf?" he asked us, more firm than angry. "Your mother told you to get inside."

Pete grabbed my shoulder and said, "C'mon."

I kept thinking about the lie I'd told Uncle Dean the night before, and how I would never get the chance to explain myself now. I felt gutted that he'd left this world believing that I was dishonest. I hated lying, and I especially hated lying for Pete, which I felt like I had to do a little too often. But it was my fault for not saying no, for not standing up to him when I knew that I should.

I kept my distance from him once inside—partly out of anger, but mostly just because I felt like I needed some space, some room of my own to breathe. That's the thing about being a little brother; you sometimes feel like you spend your whole life just orbiting around your older sibling, as if you're a satellite instead of a planet in your own right.

Had Uncle Dean ever felt that way about Dad? If so, it never showed. They'd always seemed to me the best of friends, but I guess things might have been different when they were younger. I stood at the window and tried to imagine them at Pete's and my ages, Dad the serious one and Uncle Dean the prankster, with maybe the kid brother getting the older one in trouble instead of the other way around. I'd never thought of them in that way before, and it just made it all hurt that much more.

A strange sense of hollowness began to creep into me, which perhaps was just my mind's way of trying to insulate me from myself, from the grief and anxiety that might have otherwise overwhelmed me, the way they appeared to be overwhelming Mom. She'd barely moved since coming inside, and every time that Pete tried to talk to her, she just shushed him and held her head, as if the noise was too much to bear.

The darkness ended up staying for more than an hour, and the power stayed off for another two hours on top of that.

Dad carried Uncle Dean's remains down into the basement, the fragments all gathered up into three different garbage bags. When he came back up a few minutes later, he was crying—not full-on sobbing or anything, but his eyes were noticeably wet and he was sniffling.

Mom seemed to snap out of it a little. She and Dad hugged for a minute before telling me and Pete to come over, too. We hugged as a family then, and I could feel Mom shaking. I wondered if she was going to be okay, if any of us were.

TWENTY-TWO

It's hard, trying to get back to normal after losing someone you love. You sort of just drift, from one room into another, and from one moment into the next, until eventually you focus your energy on something random, because you need to, because it hurts too much to be idle and just keep thinking about it.

It took some convincing, but I finally managed to get Pete to put down his radio and play a card game with me. I suggested UNO, but it was War that sealed the deal, most likely because Pete had a habit of ending up with most of the face cards and aces, although not this time, or at least not after the first game.

Pete took me down in a close one to start off with, but then I thoroughly trounced him in the second game, forcing a rubber match, which we were halfway through when Dad got a call from Constable Sheery that he had to respond to. Dad didn't say what it was about (he never did), but it was clear from the look on his face as he rushed out the door that it must be serious.

"Let's finish this later," said Pete. "I wanna see if something's happening."

"Nothing's happening," I told him. "Let's just play."

We had just finished a double showdown in which I'd managed to steal two jacks and an ace from Pete's pile. I had a sneaking suspicion that if we didn't finish the game now, we'd never get back to it. Most likely our cards would end up getting mysteriously mixed up while I wasn't looking.

Pete huffed and flipped over a nine to my queen.

"I hate this game," he said. "I don't even know why I play it."

He kept looking over at the stairs, as if the radio

weren't just on his mind now but actually exerting a pull on his body, like some sort of mind-control tractor beam. He was scared that he might be missing something important. That's why he hadn't wanted to play cards in the first place.

"So what if you miss something?" I'd asked him. "What's the big deal?"

"I just hate not knowing," he'd said.

We flipped again, Pete's one and only ace taking my four of diamonds.

"What a waste," he said, disgusted.

It went on for a while, as war often does, but eventually I triumphed, taking Pete's last cards in an epic triple showdown.

"Finally," said Pete, as if I'd been dragging the game out on purpose or something.

Dad arrived home right after we finished but didn't immediately come inside. Instead he sat in his truck for a few minutes, the way he used to when he still smoked cigarettes. Had he started again?

"I'll kill him," said Mom, whose thoughts were obviously running parallel to my own. She opened the front door and stood there with her arms crossed, waiting. I figured she'd start giving him the third degree as soon as he walked in the door, but she didn't, and as soon as I saw the look on Dad's face, I understood why. Something was wrong.

"What is it?" Mom asked him. "What happened?"

"It's George Crandall," said Dad.

"He shattered, didn't he?" said Pete.

Dad shook his head, real slow-like.

"What, then?" Mom asked him.

"He came back," said Dad. "He came back to his body."

"What?!" said Pete.

"Came back?" said Mom. She looked confused, like she couldn't square Dad's graveness with what should have been good news. I was confused, too. Didn't we *want* people to come back? Wasn't that what we were waiting for? But then I realized that old man Crandall must be different somehow. He must have changed, and not in a good way.

"I couldn't get him to talk," said Dad. "I tried, but I'm not even sure he *can* talk. He was just sitting there in the dark, staring at nothing. I snapped my fingers right in front of him and he didn't even look at me. Marge says he's been like that since this morning, when she found him. The only way she can get him to react at all is by turning the lights on."

"What's he do then?" I asked.

"He screams," said Dad. "Covers his eyes up and screams like a bloody banshee."

Mom gasped. "Why on earth would he do that?"

Dad shook his head. "It's just the light. Apparently he's scared of it."

Nobody said anything for a moment. But then I had to ask, "Why would he be scared of light?" If he was returning from a place of darkness, wouldn't light be something to welcome?

"I have no idea," said Dad.

"Maybe he'll get better," said Mom. "Maybe he just needs some time to settle back in."

"Maybe," said Dad. "For Marge's sake, I hope you're right."

I hoped so, too, and not just for Mrs. Crandall's sake either, because if Mr. Crandall had come back, it meant that others could come back, too, possibly in the same condition. There was a chance it had already happened and we just hadn't heard about it yet.

We turned on the TV to find out, and the headline immediately confirmed it: HUNDREDS RETURN WORLDWIDE.

"I knew it!" said Pete. "I knew something was happening!"

The ones who'd come back were all like old man Crandall, just shells of their former selves, empty eyed and helpless. None of them were talking, and they all shared a fear of the light.

"Where have they been all this time?" reporters were asking. "What happened to them, and why are they back now? Are they dangerous?"

"Dangerous?" said Mom. "Why are they asking that?" She turned to Dad. "Did George look dangerous to you?"

Dad shook his head. "I don't think he's coherent enough to be dangerous."

"Did he look different at all?" Pete asked him. "I read a story once about someone who saw the devil and it turned all his hair white."

“His hair was *already* white,” I reminded him.

“I *know*,” said Pete. “But it could’ve fallen out or something.”

“He looked the same,” said Dad. “Just…empty.”

“Please stay with us,” a reporter went on. “We’ve just received word that a New York hypnotist is attempting to regress one of the returned, and we’re expecting a statement shortly.”

“What does *regress* mean?” I asked.

“It means they’re trying to make the person remember,” said Dad. “And if they remember, then maybe they’ll talk.”

“Is that really a good idea?” asked Mom. “I mean, do we even *want* to know?”

“I think we have to know,” Dad replied. “Whether we want to or not.”

“Turn it up,” said Pete.

Five minutes went by, then ten, and finally twenty, but there was still no word from the hypnotist. People began to wonder if something had gone wrong during the session. They suggested that the police should go in to check.

I chewed my fingernails to the quick—a nervous habit of mine—but it didn’t help. My whole body thrummed with anticipation. I wasn't sure what I was expecting, exactly, but I figured it would have to be big.

The hypnotist we were waiting for was apparently a famous one who traveled all over the world using hypnotism to help people get over their fears. I didn't recognize his name at all (Dr. Norman Whitcombe), but from the picture they showed of him, his face seemed sort of familiar. He had a small chin and wore wire-rimmed spectacles, and when he finally came out of the high-rise building where he had done the regression, he was immediately swarmed by the media, who all started shouting different questions at the same time.

Dr. Whitcombe just stood there for a moment, blinking his beady eyes and waiting for the noise to settle, which it eventually did, but not before one final question rang out above all the rest: "Did he say anything?"

"Yes," Dr. Whitcombe replied, "he spoke."

There was another eruption of noise and a fresh new volley of questions. They all wanted to know what he'd said.

"He said a number of things," the doctor began. "But I think it's important for us to understand that there may have been hallucinations or dreams, and that some of the things he said may not be—and probably aren't, for that matter—rooted in reality."

The reporters were growing impatient. They wanted answers, not preamble. "Just tell us!" one of them yelled.

"Well," the doctor said uncertainly, adjusting his spectacles, "he appears to have memories of some other existence. A rather grim existence. He whispered of rivers of tar and of trees that leak blood like sap."

A stunned silence fell over the crowd.

Dr. Whitcombe cleared his throat and continued. "As I was trying to say, this imagery may have been influenced by dreams or hallucinations. At this point, it's impossible for me to say with any degree of certainty. Now, if you'll raise your hands, I'll try to get to as many questions as I can."

Every hand went up. Dr. Whitcombe pointed to a pretty reporter in a bright red blouse. "Yes?"

"Do you think it's possible that he may have actually *been* somewhere else? This grim place you mentioned?"

"It's possible," Dr. Whitcombe replied. "Or part of him, at least. His consciousness maybe, or his soul. Please keep in mind that this is pure speculation, based on answers that were largely unintelligible." He pointed to a different reporter and said, "You."

"What do you mean by *unintelligible*?" the man asked.

"Just that," the doctor replied. "The patient wavered between moments of brief lucidity and total recalcitrance. Much of what he said was gibberish. However, there were a few revealing sentences—fragmentary, mind you, but revealing. It's also clear to me that the patient has suffered a severe trauma. He was very confused."

"Confused about what?" another reporter asked without being called on.

"Everything," the doctor replied. "He moved his tongue around in his mouth as if he were no longer accustomed to having one, and at one point he failed to recognize his own hands. When I asked him what seemed unfamiliar about them, he blurted out 'small' and 'fleshy.' He then very clearly asked me what had become of all his scales."

"I'm sorry," said the closest reporter, looking bewildered, "but did you say *scales*? Like on a snake, or . . . ?"

"That's correct," Dr. Whitcombe replied. "Unfortunately, the patient would elucidate no further."

Pete and I shared a look, then simultaneously turned our gazes on Mom, who had lost all color in her face.

“He must be lying,” she said.

Dr. Norman Whitcombe looked genuine to me, though, and more than that, he seemed genuinely troubled at having to be the one to share the unsettling news. Nevertheless, many of the reporters appeared to agree with Mom. They started asking about Dr. Whitcombe’s methods instead of his results. Some of them even went so far as to suggest that this whole endeavor must be a hoax, a publicity stunt of the very worst kind.

“I assure you it’s not,” Dr. Whitcombe tried to tell them, but now that the idea had been planted, it seemed to take root.

“I bet the regression didn’t even work!” said one of them.

“How dare you!” said another.

Sensing a dangerous shift, Norman Whitcombe began to back away. I think he was just about to turn and run when someone who apparently did believe him asked: “How is the patient now?”

“The same as before the regression,” the doctor replied. “Unreachable.”

It was the last thing he would say on the matter.

Unreachable. The word stuck with me. It seemed to imply that something had either been lost or left behind, perhaps permanently.

Pete was stuck on a different word, though.

"Scales," he said, with a mixture of wonder and fear. He looked down at his own hands then, as if trying to imagine what that would look like.

"I can't believe it," said Mom. "How could that be?"

Dad just shook his head, as if he was past the point of trying to make sense of anything.

I didn't know what to think, but my mind kept going back to that Polaroid photo, to that eerie human-shaped figure, fuzzy as if seen through a fog, or perhaps through the curtain separating this reality from a different one.

Maybe the change in the sky signaled a sort of convergence, an overlapping of worlds that left us vulnerable. What if Dr. Whitcombe was right when he said that it might have been his patient's soul that had traveled somewhere else? I'd always thought that our souls couldn't leave our bodies unless we died, but maybe that wasn't true. Maybe we just needed to be put in a state that was *like* death. Maybe then our souls would come unglued. Maybe then they could be taken.

I imagined the blurry photograph figure as a stealer of souls, a scale-covered demon exploiting some cosmic loophole that Satan had somehow stumbled upon and was now taking advantage of. Maybe the world converging with ours was hell itself.

I shuddered at the thought, then told myself I was being stupid, and that my imagination was just running away on me (as it often did). The idea sort of made sense, though. As much as anything else did.

TWENTY-THREE

Two more days passed, making it four since Uncle Dean had come down from the roof. Constable Sheery conducted a census throughout town and, according to him, thirty-six people turned to glass at the same time as Uncle Dean. Twenty-five of them were still solid and whole, but the rest had all since shattered. None had come back to their bodies.

Constable Sheery said that the youngest of them was only seventeen. This was one year older than the youngest person known to have turned to glass so far. Apparently kids were safe from it; however, nobody really knew why. Pete said that the guy on the radio believed it was because young people were still too innocent and pure, that they hadn't yet been weakened by "accumulated sin," which I guess just meant that they hadn't done enough bad things yet, although most of the adults I knew weren't bad either. Maybe small sins counted, too, things like little white lies and occasional moments of selfishness and greed. Maybe it all added up to something bigger.

I wasn't sure what to believe. I thought of the Messam twins and wondered if maybe they were vulnerable, too, in spite of their age. I hoped so, otherwise the whole planet might end up becoming like that island in *Lord of the Flies*, with guys like Lars and Lester ruling the roost. I didn't like my odds in a world like that. Conch shell or no conch shell, I doubted anyone would have much use for the opinion of an eleven-year-old birder.

"Pastor Nolan is holding a special service this Sunday," Dad told us. "He's going to be remembering everyone who has shattered in Griever's Mill."

"Like a funeral?" I asked him.

"Sort of," said Dad.

"Is he gonna talk about Uncle Dean?"

Dad nodded. The bags under his eyes were getting darker, and I knew that he hadn't been sleeping much, because I hadn't heard him snoring. His back was bugging him, too, probably from all the wood-chopping he'd been doing. I thought Pete had gotten carried away with the ax a few days before, but that was nothing compared to Dad. Twice now he'd been out there for hours at a time, splitting logs as if his life depended on it, the neighborhood echoing with every impact of metal on wood. Mom was worried about him, that he was going to give himself a heart attack.

"We'll probably be the only ones there," said Pete. At church, he meant.

Lots of people in town had begun to leave, some with trucks and trailers crammed to capacity, and others with only their cars and whatever they could fit inside them and on their roofs, precarious towers of overstuffed luggage and hastily packed boxes, tied down with so many bungee cords and bright orange ratchet straps.

"Where are they going?" I had asked Dad.

"To be with friends and family," Dad had replied. "While they still have the gas to get to them."

Pete had another theory, though. "They think they'll be safer away from town, for when things get worse."

"Worse how?" I asked him.

"Food shortages," he said. "It's already happening in some places. It's gonna be every man for himself."

"No it isn't," said Dad with a scowl of disapproval.

Pete shrugged as if to say that he knew differently, which maybe he did. He'd been listening to his radio pretty much nonstop and was probably sleeping even less than Dad was.

"It doesn't matter who will or won't be there," Dad continued. "We're going to put on our Sunday best and give thanks to the Lord just like always."

"Thanks for what?" Pete asked.

Pete had never been fond of church and had never made much effort in hiding it either. I felt the same a lot of the time—especially on sunny mornings when I could be watching birds or riding my bike instead—but I knew that it was important to Dad, so I tried not to complain.

"For accepting your uncle Dean into heaven," said Mom as she walked into the room.

That shut Pete up pretty much instantly.

"I miss him," I said into the silence that followed. I kept remembering how he was always adjusting his ball cap and how the smell of the garage clung to him no matter where he went, an oddly comforting mixture of metal and grease.

"We all do, Ben," Dad told me. "We all do." He smiled a sad sort of smile, then swallowed hard and blinked his eyes a few times, fighting off tears. He cleared his throat. "I'm going to go over to his garage and grab a few things," he said. "I shouldn't be more than an hour."

It was usually a given that when Dad went anywhere, Pete would ask if he could go with him, but not today. Pete didn't say anything at all. I think he just wanted to get back to his radio. I offered to go, but Dad shook his head.

"I think I'll just go on my own this time, okay, champ?"

"Okay," I replied. It occurred to me then that maybe Dad needed some time on his own to deal with his pain, to let it out where no one could see him. I think Mom realized that, too, because she let him go without an argument, after which she returned to her regular spot at the kitchen window, where it seemed she could stand indefinitely without moving or speaking. I wanted to believe that she was just watching birds, but I suspected that she wasn't really watching anything at all. She was just staring, at everything and nothing all at once.

As expected, Pete returned to our room and his whispering speaker, leaving me alone on the living room floor, in front of a muted TV that I was starting to hate.

TWENTY-FOUR

It was closer to two hours before Dad got back. His eyes were red and his shoulders slumped, and he looked like a man defeated.

Among the things he'd brought back with him were a big toolbox and a crate full of Uncle Dean's personal things, clothes and knickknacks and whatnot. He'd also hauled over all the wood from behind the garage, where Uncle Dean had a firepit and two long benches that he and Dad and some of their friends used to sit on while drinking beer and talking about sports and fishing and who knows what else (probably women).

Pete and I weren't allowed there. The firepit area had always been an adult-only zone.

"There are work gloves on the backseat," Dad told Pete and me. "You can help me unload this."

Mom stood in the driveway with her arms crossed. "I think we have enough wood already, don't we?"

"Not if we end up having to burn it all winter," Dad replied.

"But it's still summer."

"And I might not be here come fall," Dad said bluntly.

"Don't say that!" Mom scolded him, as if bringing it up was to tempt fate.

"It's just the truth, Jane."

It was also true that Mom might be gone by then, too.

"I don't care if it's the truth," said Mom. "I don't want you talking like that."

Dad looked at her for a second but didn't say anything. He lowered a particularly large chunk of wood down to Pete. "Careful with this one," he said. "It's heavy."

"I got it," Pete assured him. He wavered a bit once the weight was fully in his arms, but then readjusted his grip and seemed okay.

"Smaller piece, please," I said. I knew I wasn't strong and saw little point in trying to prove otherwise.

"Here," said Dad. "And don't bother piling them neatly. I'm going to chop them all right away."

"You haven't even had lunch yet," said Mom. It was just after one.

"I had a beer and some jerky at the garage," said Dad.

Uncle Dean had *loved* beef jerky and always kept some of it around. I think the only thing he loved more was homemade shepherd's pie. He came over whenever Mom made it and would sometimes park himself at the table an hour or more in advance, as if supper were a concert that he had to wait in line to get tickets for. I remembered coming home from school one day to find him sitting there with a fork in one hand and a knife in the other, and the food not even in the oven yet. Being there early was just his way of showing his appreciation. That's the kind of man Uncle Dean had been.

Mom looked like she might say something else, but instead just turned and went back in the house. Dad watched her go, a weird tension left hanging in the air. Pete and I stayed to help finish unloading, and then we went inside as well. A few minutes later, Dad had the ax in his hand and a log on the chopping block. He stood there for a moment just staring at it, as if he was no longer sure he had the strength to bother. His shoulders rose as he took a deep breath, then lowered as he let it out slow. He did this a couple more times, and then he began.

He went easy to start with, but it wasn't long before he was moving at a frenzied pace, and even then he kept trying to go faster and swing even harder, as if there were some sort of threshold he needed to cross, a way of erasing the past and fixing the future through sheer exhaustion. He looked possessed.

Mom stood in the doorway, looking out at him and shaking her head as if to say, *Here we go again.*

It was different this time, though. He wasn't just getting it all out like a boxer at a body bag, channeling his stress through the head of an ax instead of his fists; he seemed desperate now. Panicked, almost.

I think we all sensed this change and that's why we all kept watching, from the first log until the last, which Dad placed on the block before pausing and looking around in sudden confusion, realizing only then that there wasn't any wood left for him to annihilate.

He roared in frustration as he brought the ax down

one last time, then dropped to his knees and started sobbing, his whole body shaking from the force of it.

"Dad!" I yelled, pressing my hand to the glass of the window.

Mom rushed out to him, calling his name. She dropped down beside him and pulled him close to her, telling him, "It's okay. Just let it all out."

Pete looked utterly devastated, like he'd just watched Superman himself plummet out of the sky and into the earth like a mortal man. As much as they were always getting under each other's skin, there was no one in the world who Pete revered more than Dad.

That moment was a turning point for Pete. Afterward, he would no longer disagree just to be disagreeable, but rather because he no longer had the faith in Dad that he once had, and because he now felt a quiet resentment for having seen something that he felt like no son should ever have to see in his father: weakness.

It didn't matter that the moment would last only minutes, and that Dad would stand up just as tall and straight as he'd ever stood before. The bricks had already been set in my brother's psyche. There was no going back.

Pete left the window and went upstairs.

"Look what you did to your hands," said Mom.

Dad blinked like a man fresh from a trance. His palms were bloody where he'd torn open calluses. The pain seemed to hit him belatedly. He winced and clenched both hands to fists.

Mom told him to come inside and clean himself up. He kept his boots on and went straight to the kitchen sink, his whole body tensing as hot water entered the cuts. He gritted his teeth, and probably bit his tongue to keep from swearing.

"Honestly," Mom said, shaking her head in admonishment.

By the time Dad toweled his hands off, he seemed wholly himself again, as if the inner storm that had been raging for days had finally blown itself out. All it took was a moment of pure surrender. He regarded me where I was sitting.

"You and Pete should get outside today," he said. "Still plenty of daylight left. Go to the pond or something. Skip some stones. Be boys."

"I don't know. . . ." said Mom.

"Would you rather them be girls?" Dad asked her, a sly smirk tugging at the corners of his lips.

"Very funny," said Mom, who clearly wasn't ready for jokes yet. Not after what had just happened.

"But seriously, Jane," Dad continued. "We can't all stay cooped up in this house forever. We'll go stir-crazy. Where is Pete, anyway?" he asked.

"Up in our room," I said, "with his radio."

"Figures," said Dad, marching off toward the stairs.

I could hear Pete complaining a moment later, saying, "But I don't want to!"

"I don't care," Dad told him. "It'll do you boys good to breathe some fresh air."

"I'll open a window," said Pete.

"You'll do as I say," Dad continued, "or I'll take that thing away from you."

There was silence for a second, then Pete came clomping down the stairs and said to me, "C'mon," as if I were a dog that he felt put out for having to walk. I knew he wasn't really mad at me, though.

A few minutes later we were on our way to the pond at the south edge of town, the one directly beside the graveyard. Tadpole Pond, we called it, because we used to catch tadpoles there when we were younger. We were going to ride our bikes, but Pete couldn't find his lock key. Pete was always losing things.

"He *better* not take it away," said Pete, obviously still thinking about his radio, and about Dad as well.

"What's with you and that radio, anyway?" I asked.

"I just like to stay on top of what's happening," he replied, a little defensively.

"So, what *is* happening?" I asked him. I only knew what I saw on TV, which always seemed to be a little behind what Pete heard on the radio.

"They're doing more regressions," said Pete. "Different hypnotists, like a dozen of them. Remember how Dr. Whitcombe said that a lot of what he heard was just gibberish?"

I nodded.

"They don't think so anymore," said Pete. "They think it's a different language. They said it might be Enochian."

"What's *Enochian*?"

"An ancient language used by angels and demons."

I just looked at him. "For real?"

Pete shrugged. "They're not sure yet. They're trying to translate."

"What else have they said?"

"Not a lot. But they're all scared of the light like old man Crandall, and one of them said something about fields full of bodies, but not human bodies. He said that crows were feasting like kings."

I felt a shiver at the imagery, but then a question sprang to mind. "Why would crows be there?"

Pete shrugged again. "Beats me."

"Is that it?" I asked.

"Not quite. The guy on the radio says that if you shatter on this side, it might be because you've died on that side. He also says that it might work the other way around. If you shatter on this side, you die over there."

I thought about that for a minute as we approached the pond, but before I could really consider how important it might be, my eyes were drawn to the tall grasses at the edge of the water, where I thought I saw something moving—a heron, perhaps, or maybe a bittern. I stopped walking and grabbed Pete's shirt to hold him back.

"What is it?" he asked.

"Not sure yet," I whispered. I should have brought Mom's binoculars. I squinted against the sun, my pulse quickening at the prospect of seeing a bird I'd never come across before. A few seconds passed, and then a few seconds more, and just as I was beginning to think that my eyes must've been playing tricks on me, there it was, a yellowish bill materializing from the reeds, followed by a long gray-and-blue neck.

"There," I whispered, pointing. The bird was almost as tall as I was.

"What the heck is that?" asked Pete, obviously surprised at the size of what he was seeing. He was used to me pointing out birds barely bigger than his hand.

"Great blue heron," I whispered. We could see its whole body now, but miraculously it hadn't noticed us yet. Its bill was pointed downward, its large reptilian eyes focused on the shallow water in which it stood. It moved methodically, clearly looking for prey. The instant it spotted something, it struck, its bill piercing down with incredible speed. It didn't come up with a fish, though, but rather a garter snake—about three feet long by the looks of it. The snake wriggled in a bid to escape, but to no avail. The bird turned its long bill skyward and, with three deft flips, had the entirety of the snake within its throat. It swallowed the serpent down with surprising ease.

I'd seen some pretty neat things while watching birds in the past, but never anything like this. I was so enthralled that I failed to notice for a second that Pete was moving.

"No, wait!" I whispered at him, but it was too late. At the sound of scuffed gravel beneath Pete's shoe, the bird turned sharply in our direction, giving us both a brief and intense stare before flying off on huge silent wings.

"Did you see that?!" Pete exclaimed. "It ate a whole blasted snake! What kind of a bird eats a snake?"

Maybe I should have been heartened by his newfound interest in nature, but instead I was angry. If he had just stayed still, we could have kept watching the bird. I felt like he'd robbed me of a rare opportunity, and the fact that he was completely oblivious to this only made me even madder.

"You can't just walk up to them!" I told him. "That's not how it works! You have to be patient. You have to move *slow.*"

Patience had never been Pete's strong suit.

"It's not like we have all day," he said. "And besides,

we already saw it eat a snake. What are the odds it was gonna do something more interesting than that?"

He had a point, but still, I was annoyed.

"That was crazy," he went on, moving forward. "I didn't even know there *were* garter snakes around here."

I'd known that there were, of course, but I hadn't actually seen one before.

Keeping to our usual ritual at the pond, we both collected a handful of rocks from the roadside before going down to the most accessible edge of the water.

"Maybe you'll skip one all the way across today," Pete said encouragingly, but I had other plans.

Pete had spent hours teaching me how to properly skip stones, and though I still wasn't very good at it, I knew that each small success I had was a source of pride for him. I could tell that it made him feel like a proper big brother.

Annoyed as I was, I decided to take that away from him today.

He took two throws first, his stones skipping six and seven times respectively.

"Not bad," he said. "Now you go."

I took my position like a pitcher on a mound, feigning

concentration. My form was almost but not quite right. My partial crouch was slightly off, and when I followed through on my toss, I angled my arm in such a way that the stone started out low as it was supposed to, but then gradually gained altitude instead of traveling level with the water. It landed with a dismal *galupe* and a modest splash.

My second throw was no better.

"Do it like I taught you!" Pete said, already irritated. "Keep your arm straight, like this." His third stone went skipping across the water, right to the other side. I counted nine bounces.

"I *am* doing it like you showed me," I insisted.

"No you're not," he argued. "You might as well just be lobbing them. Here, use this one."

He handed me a particularly good candidate, oblong and thin but still substantial enough to get a firm grip on. I thanked him and pretended to limber up a little, really laying it on thick now. It was all I could do to keep a straight face as this stone, too, disappeared without a single skip.

Pete huffed derisively. "Here, I'll do an impression of you." He picked up the biggest, roundest rock in the vicinity and heaved it out over the water from between his legs, like a rookie with a bowling ball. It sailed high into the air before falling to the surface just a few feet away from me, the heavy *sploosh* sending a spray of droplets in my direction. He laughed.

I wiped off my face and looked at him. "Now you're just being stupid."

"Stupid is not being able to skip a rock," he shot back.

"You don't have to get mad," I told him. "I am trying."

"Barely." He shook his head and proceeded to skip six rocks in quick succession, as if trying to demonstrate how little effort it actually took. Meanwhile, I managed to find myself a mini boulder, fully twice the size of the one Pete had thrown from between his legs. Pete didn't even see it until it was right in front of him, plummeting to the earth like a burned-up meteorite.

The splash it made was bigger than I would have thought possible.

"What the heck did you do that for?!" he yelled at me, dirty water dripping from his chin.

"You did it first" was my only reply.

"I barely even got you wet!" he said. "Look at me! My clothes are soaked!"

They were. I'd really gotten him good. I couldn't

hold it in anymore; I had to smile. And then suddenly I was laughing, too, the sound escaping from my mouth like a wild animal freed from a cage. I hadn't laughed in days, and I immediately felt its healing power course through me, soaking my anger up like a sponge.

Pete's face contorted in a way that I had only ever seen in Incredible Hulk comics, but this only got me laughing harder. Glee was a possessive force and had taken me over. I was helpless against it.

Luckily, Pete succumbed, too. Like invisible lightning, the need for laughter seemed to arc from me to him, and all at once his features softened, his rage subsiding as quickly as it had appeared. A moment later we were both doubled over, and a moment after that was when the mud-flinging started. Pete got me first, a soggy handful that filled my ear. I quickly got my revenge with a pinpoint blob that plugged up both of his nostrils. Then things got a little out of control.

It never occurred to us that when we got home, Mom would make us wash our clothes ourselves, and not with the regular washing machine either, but rather with the basin and washboard that Dad had gotten his hands on for when the power was out. But even if that had occurred to me, I wouldn't have cared. I couldn't remember the last time I'd laughed so hard that the muscles in my jaw got sore.

We walked home like a pair of swamp creatures fresh from the ooze.

TWENTY-FIVE

Sunday marked our seventh day in a row without any darkness, which meant that Griever's Mill was probably one of the luckiest places on earth.

Pete and I laced up our good leather shoes after having spent twenty minutes polishing them to perfection, Pete complaining almost the entire time.

"If we're going to walk there, then why bother polishing our shoes?" he'd said. "They're just going to end up getting scuffed on the way."

"Don't drag your feet and they'll be fine," Dad told him. "And no fidgeting today," he added. Pete had a habit of rolling up hymn books and using them as hollow drumsticks against his knees and the edge of the pew, and sometimes the back of Kyle Brewer's head if Kyle happened to be at church that day. (Dad said that Kyle's parents were on-again, off-again Christians.) Pete also liked to tap his feet and crack his knuckles. I don't think he could even help it; his basic wiring just didn't allow for him to keep still. Unless of course he had a radio pressed to his ear.

"I'm not the only one who fidgets," Pete grumbled. Pete hated being singled out, never mind that there was usually a very good reason for it.

"Just promise me," said Dad.

"Fine," said Pete. "I'll just sit there, then." As if sitting were a form of punishment.

"Hallelujah," said Dad. "Everybody ready?"

I did up the last button on my shirt cuff and nodded. I had mixed feelings about church today. It was going to be hard, hearing about Uncle Dean and all the other victims who Pastor Nolan planned to eulogize. I expected there to be a lot of crying. However, I also expected the pastor to say a few things about the glass plague, and what it might mean from his perspective. I figured that if scientists couldn't make heads nor tails of what was happening, then maybe a pastor could—not that I'd ever been much of a spiritual person myself. My faith seemed to depend entirely on how I was feeling and what was going on at any particular moment. Perhaps that made me an on-again, off-again Christian, too.

For Uncle Dean's sake, I hoped it all wasn't just a load of crazy superstition. The idea that consciousness could end so suddenly and permanently didn't seem fair to me.

"I don't understand why we can't just drive," Pete persisted. "It'll hardly take any gas at all."

"It's a beautiful day outside," Mom said to him. "It'll be nice to take a walk as a family. Besides, *I'm* the one wearing heels. If anyone should be complaining, it should be me."

Pete didn't seem to have anything to say to that, and so off we went.

In truth, it was only about a fifteen-minute walk, which was pretty much the same amount of time that it took for Pete and me to get to school (when we didn't ride our bikes). And Mom was right—as long as you weren't thinking about where you were going or why you were going there, it really was a beautiful day. The sun was shining and there was hardly any wind at all. Lots of birdsong as well. Mom and I took turns identifying them by sound as we went.

"American goldfinch," she began.

"Gray catbird," I added a moment later. Catbirds were amazing singers, but at this time of the year they were usually just making their mewling cat sounds.

"Cedar waxwing," Mom went on. There were actually about twenty of them, scattered across the tops of two different trees. I watched them for a moment as we walked, saw them catching small insects in midair.

I listened hard, ignoring a few of the more common birds in the hopes of picking out something a little more difficult.

"Tennessee warbler," I finally came up with.

Mom smiled. "Good one!" she said. It was nice to see her so lively and bright-eyed.

Pete cocked an ear then, too, mocking me in a way that was simultaneously playful and serious, so that I couldn't tell if he was genuinely trying to hurt my feelings or not. "Ruby-breasted spinker," he declared, which of course wasn't a real bird.

I shook my head and rolled my eyes. Mom decided to play along.

"Oh, yeah? And what sound does a ruby-breasted spinker make?" she asked him.

Pete rocked his shoulders and searched the sky for a second before coming up with the obvious, "Spink-spink."

"Sounds kind of like a least flycatcher," I informed him.

Mom and Dad both laughed, but Pete just called me a geek. I didn't care. I was used to it.

We arrived at the church a few minutes later to find that the parking lot was almost half-full, this despite the fact that so many people had left Griever's Mill altogether.

Mom took a deep breath, steeling herself.

On the church's front lawn, facing the street, was one of those signs that you could slide letters into to spell out messages. I read what it said every time we came to church. Occasionally, they would put direct Bible quotes on it, but often the message was something simple, like WELCOME, ONE AND ALL! or DO UNTO OTHERS... but today it read, REMEMBER: IT'S ALWAYS DARKEST JUST BEFORE THE DAWN.

Maybe this was supposed to make us all feel a little better, but instead it made me feel worse. After all, the darkness was still coming and going all over the world. Would it have to be complete before things got better?

Several people stopped to offer condolences as we went inside. "Dean will be missed," one of them said. "He was quite a character," another added. A third said, "Best mechanic I ever knew. The absolute best."

Dad just said thank you each time. Mom didn't say anything. I could tell that she knew that she'd cry if she opened her mouth. She had that look on her face, her eyes downcast, lips a little pursed to keep them from trembling.

We quickly learned that Charlie Watts had shattered, too, just the night before. Pete shook his head in disbelief as we shuffled to our usual spot in the seventh row and sat down. Mrs. Crandall was in her usual spot as well, but of course George wasn't. Mom patted the old woman's knee to let her know that she cared.

"How is George?" she asked her.

"The same," Mrs. Crandall said sadly. "I figured it couldn't hurt to come pray."

Pastor Nolan started by thanking us all for coming,

and for finding the strength to be there for one another during these hard times. He went on to say that from misfortune can come fortitude, and that the human spirit is possessed of an uncanny propensity to overcome. His voice carried effortlessly throughout the large space even though he didn't seem to be speaking that loudly. I'd mentioned this before and, according to Dad, it was down to good acoustics.

"I know that many of you are here because you've lost loved ones," the pastor said, "and I know that many of you are seeking answers as to why, but I think it's important for us not to become too consumed by the need for understanding, for while it may seem to us sometimes that the Lord might revel in the inexplicable, we have to remind ourselves that His plan is larger than any of us, and by its very nature, wholly inexplicable."

He paused, allowing everyone a moment to digest his words, or at least a moment to *try* to digest his words. It wasn't always easy with Pastor Nolan.

"But let us also remember," he went on, "that our faith requires no recognition on the part of the Lord. Faith is a leap we all make in the darkness, a trust that endures in the seeming absence of His light. But make no mistake, His light is here, all around us, bleeding out in every kindness, in every smile and small act of love. And so love we must, with every fiber of our being, with every atom and every cell. Only then will His will be done. Now let us stand and sing...."

Organ music filled the room as I picked up a hymn book. It's funny; whenever there's a church scene in a movie or on a TV show, it's always a little old lady playing the organ. Usually she's got big Coke-bottle glasses on and is wearing a knit sweater of some kind, and she always looks like she belongs there, like the bench was made especially for her. Our church didn't have a little old lady. Ours had a giant of a man with a long thick beard and huge Paul Bunyan hands. By rights he should have been out in the woods with an ax, felling trees like a plaid-wrapped tornado, but instead he was sporting slacks and a pale blue dress shirt, his meaty fingers gentle on the ivory keys. The bench looked comical beneath him, and the organ seemed strangely miniaturized, as if he'd sat down to bang away at Schroeder's toy piano.

The big man was Pastor Nolan's son, Patrick, and though you never would have known it to see the two of them together (Pastor Nolan wasn't very big himself), if you got up close and really looked, you'd see that their eyes were exactly the same hazel color and that their noses were a match as well. I'm pretty good at spotting distinguishing features like that. I think it's probably because I draw a lot, and with drawing you have to get the proportions just right, otherwise nothing looks like it's supposed to.

Pastor Nolan's son was an artist, too—not a drawer like me, but a painter, a really well-known painter. He mostly did nature-scapes, usually with animals like foxes or cougars or wolves. *Especially* wolves. There was an art gallery in Paulson that actually had one whole section devoted to Patrick's work. We took a school trip there once to see it. Most of my classmates seemed bored by the exhibit, but I thought it was awesome. They even gave us all a free five-by-seven print at the end of the tour, of a lynx in a snowstorm. I got a cheap frame for mine and hung it up on the wall near my closet.

Mom and Dad both said that if I kept at it, my art could end up in a gallery someday, too. I wasn't so sure. As far as I could tell, they didn't put pencil drawings up in galleries, and the only paintbrush I'd ever held was for a crappy watercolor I did way back in first grade.

The hymn we were singing was one I'd sung before. I knew most of the words, so I only had to look down at the book occasionally. Mostly I was looking at everyone else, checking the pews for other kids I knew. Kyle Brewer and his parents weren't there, so I guessed they either were "off-again" or had maybe packed up and left.

I was glad to see that some of my classmates were still around. Claude Lafleur was two rows over, sitting with his mom, who was always one of the loudest (and best) singers in church. I waited for a moment until he looked my way, at which point we exchanged subtle salutes. That was kind of our thing, and had been since we were little on account of the mini green army battles we so often staged in Claude's huge sandbox. Saluting was a show of respect from one general to another. Claude was a short kid and liked to speak French on the battlefield, which always made him sound sort of maniacal. All he needed was one of those crazy bicorne hats and he could have been a modern-day Napoleon Bonaparte.

Sitting in the pew just in front of Claude was Jeremy Kaskill, who was known as the kid who would follow through on pretty much any dare, no matter how crazy or dangerous. He cracked three ribs once while bumper hitching our school bus just before Christmas break, which you would think might have made him reconsider his risk-taking ways, but it never did. A few months later he lost six teeth while attempting a back-flip on his shiny new BMX. The ramp he'd been using was subsequently confiscated and burned by Constable Sheery. Jeremy and I got along just fine at school, but we didn't hang out together or anything. That was pretty much the case with most of the kids I knew. I had friends; they just weren't full-time friends.

Stacia Pittman was at church as well. Stacia was in Pete's grade, not mine, but everyone knew who she was because of her recent growth spurt. She'd gotten so used to boys staring at her that I think she'd developed sort of a Spidey-sense about it. She turned her head and caught me immediately.

I quickly looked down, feeling my face redden with embarrassment. Then the whispers and gasps started.

For a second I thought that I was the cause, that my wandering eyes had earned me the ire of not only Stacia Pittman but of every other girl and woman in the vicinity, which of course was ridiculous. There was no way more than a few of them could've noticed, and even if they had, why would they care? I was just a boy looking at a girl—nothing earth-shattering about that.

The one thing that they definitely *would* have noticed, though—and cared about as well—was the sudden darkening of the church.

"Uh-oh," said Pete.

I belatedly looked up through the church's huge skylight windows, and into a now-familiar coal-smoke darkness.

Some of the whispers grew to shouts then, but not before the loud and discordant plink of several misstruck organ keys momentarily silenced the room. The hymn ended just like that, on those last few unfortunate notes, completely out of tune, and even before I looked over at Patrick and the organ, I knew exactly why.

The big man on his miniature bench had turned to glass.

Chaos erupted through the whole room, which, due to the loss of power, was even darker now than it had been a moment before. People started yelling and screaming and running down the aisles. Not Mom, though. Mom just slowly sat back down, quiet as a mouse, as if stillness alone might keep her safe in the blackness. She'd been having such a good day.

"Easy now," said Mrs. Crandall to anyone close enough to hear her. "Let's all stay calm now. Let's all just breathe." Maybe it was because she'd gone through this all before, or maybe it was just because she was used to the dark now that Mr. Crandall had returned and didn't like the lights on, but for whatever reason, the old woman's voice was as steady as a rock.

I actually did hear Mom take a breath in response to her words, and then another one, but although her mind might be seeking the calm that Mrs. Crandall had asked for, her body had other ideas. The long deep breaths seemed to trigger a series of short and shallow ones. All at once Mom was hyperventilating.

"Mom?" I said. "Mom, are you okay?"

Her eyes were wide, her chest rising and falling too quickly.

"C'mon," said Mrs. Crandall, looking at Dad now. "Let's get her downstairs, away from all this commotion."

Downstairs was where everyone always went after Sunday service was over. They would put out coffee and baked goods and everyone would just stand around chatting and laughing for a while before going home. We usually only stayed for fifteen minutes or so. I don't think Dad ever really wanted to stay at all (the reason he went to church had more to do with faith than it did community) but felt like we should just for appearance's sake. That, or he couldn't resist the butter tarts, which had always been his favorite, and Pete's favorite as well. My personal weakness was for the peanut butter and marshmallow squares.

Together, Dad and Mrs. Crandall managed to get Mom out into the main aisle, and from there to the stairwell itself. Pete and I followed behind, or at least we started to. I only made it as far as the end of our pew before I glanced up at the skylight above, where a section of blue sky now competed for space with the darkness.

I'd seen this all before, of course—sunlight returning as blackness moved off—but this time the illusion of safety was undone by the knowledge that even in the house of God, we weren't really safe at all.

I think Pastor Nolan might have come to the same conclusion himself, as he loosened his white-knuckled grip on his leather-bound Bible and simply let it fall to the floor, where it landed with the force of a brick, the cover closing with an eerie finality, like a hardening layer of snow in the wake of an avalanche.

I looked down at it, that huge volume, and wondered about the colors of the page markers left within and what they meant. Had the pastor marked certain passages for certain people? Like maybe blue markers for Charlie Watts and orange for Uncle Dean? Would we ever know?

I stared at our white-robed minister and waited for him to say something, anything, but when he finally opened his mouth, only two words came out.

"Oh, Patrick..." he said, as if his son were six years old and had just spilled milk on the kitchen floor. Patrick still had his hands over the keys, his shiny black fingers just brushing the brilliant white ivory.

Pastor Nolan finally went over to him, and somehow found enough room on the little bench to sit down beside him.

"What are you doing?" said Pete, who had come back to get me. He grabbed my arm and gave it a yank. "C'mon."

I allowed myself to be pulled, my eyes sweeping the room as I went. Patrick wasn't alone, I realized. Poor

Stacia was sobbing hysterically, her mom on one side of her and her dad on the other, both of them now as hard and immovable as the heavy wood pews beneath their glass bodies.

"Come back!" she was saying, tears streaming down her face. "Come back! Come back!" She yanked at her father's arm as if trying to force him to stand, and when that didn't work, she grabbed her mom by the shoulders in a futile attempt to shake her back to reality. It was one of the saddest and strangest things I would ever see, and I was relieved when someone finally stepped in and pulled Stacia away, wrapping her up in a heartbreaking hug. It was her aunt, I think, or maybe a family friend.

I couldn't believe that both of her parents had been taken at once. It seemed cruel beyond all reason, and it forced me to face the possibility that the same thing could happen to me. I guess I'd already known that it could, but only in a distant way. Seeing it play out right in front of me made it all seem suddenly real. Too real.

I had to look away. Only then did I notice that old Deiter Brooks, who coached high school football, had turned to glass as well. A young woman, who I knew by appearance but not by name, looked to be the fifth and final victim.

Mom's breathing was almost normal again by the time I got downstairs. Dad and Mrs. Crandall both looked relieved, and I guess Pete did, too, but he also seemed a bit annoyed, at me, maybe, for lagging behind, but maybe not. I couldn't help but notice that there wasn't a single butter tart to be had.

TWENTY-SIX

We left the church as soon as Mom felt up to it. Mrs. Crandall offered to drive us home in her nut-brown Lincoln Town Car, which was definitely the biggest car in town, and possibly the biggest I'd ever seen. We were just about to pile in when I saw that there were crows outside. A few flew off with strident caws as soon as I noticed them, but one remained, perched on the church's slide-letter sign like a black-winged gargoyle—a very disheveled-looking gargoyle. There were feathers sticking out this way and that, and a few of them missing from its tail as well. It looked like it had flown through a hurricane, or had just returned from some perilous journey to who knows where.

“Look,” I said to Mom, but her head was already turning. That’s how it is with longtime birders; they notice birds even when they’re not trying to. Their brains just become wired to seek out bird shapes in any environment. The crow stared back at us for a moment, then pumped its wings like a bellows and scolded us roundly before hopping to the end of the sign and launching itself into the air. It only made it about ten or twelve feet before falling back to the ground.

Mom took a step toward it. “I think it’s hurt.”

“C’mon, you two,” Dad told us.

“Wait,” I said.

“It’s only a crow,” Dad continued. “C’mon.”

“We can’t just leave it if it’s hurt,” Mom replied. She seemed to have forgotten that just minutes before she’d been hyperventilating in a room full of panicked churchgoers.

“For heaven’s sake, Jane!” said Dad. “I think we have bigger things to worry about right now.”

“Its eyes aren’t blue,” Mom went on, ignoring him entirely, “so it’s definitely not a juvenile.”

Unfledged juveniles can sometimes look scruffy, so that's why she would've been looking at the bird's eyes. *Unfledged* was just another way of saying "not ready to fly yet," which this bird obviously should have been. The crow remained where it had landed a moment earlier, in the grass along a hedgerow. It continued to watch us warily.

Mom tried to get closer but the bird seemed to be able to hop all right. It moved to the edge of the grass where the hedgerow met the sidewalk.

"I'm sure it's fine, dear," said Mrs. Crandall. "It probably just doesn't want to fly right now."

Mom still didn't look convinced, so Dad took it upon himself to find out one way or another, and he ran at the bird and shouted while clapping his hands.

"Go on!" he yelled. "Get!"

The crow cawed and took an awkward running start down the sidewalk before flapping its shabby-looking wings and attempting liftoff for a second time. This time it succeeded in staying airborne, but only just. It looked like a bird that was trying to fly while carrying something too heavy, only there wasn't anything in the crow's talons at all. It was flying solo. I watched as it struggled to make it first over the church and then over the fence and the row of pine trees beyond, at which point it disappeared from view.

Mom shot Dad a harsh glare. "I don't think *that* was really necessary."

"Let's go home" was Dad's only reply.

And so we did, the four of us piling into Mrs. Crandall's car without another word. My thoughts kept going back and forth between the haggard crow and the image of Patrick on his bench. Crows were sometimes seen as bad omens, but they were also considered lucky. It all depended on where you looked or who you asked.

That's the thing with crows and ravens: The more you learn about them, the more you realize just how much there *is* to learn about them. It isn't just facts and observations like it is with so many other birds; there are legends, too, and entire mythologies. I did a school report on them one time and it ended up being fifteen pages long even though our teacher said it only had to be five. There was just too much stuff that I felt like I couldn't leave out.

Native Americans had dozens of stories about ravens and crows, some of them making the birds out to be troublemakers, while others depicted them as saviors or symbols of strength and wisdom. There was one story about naughty kids being turned into crows (though I couldn't remember why), and another about a rainbow-colored crow that brought fire to keep people warm, charring its own feathers black in the process.

In Celtic and Irish mythology, gods and goddesses sometimes took on the form of a crow or raven (often on the battlefield), and in Norse mythology, the god Odin relied on his two pet ravens, Huginn and Muninn (the names meant "thought" and "desire"), to fly all over the world and bring him back important information.

There were stories about the clever black birds from almost every place and culture around the world, but probably the most common legend I found was the one about crows and ravens carrying human souls from this world into the next one, as if the border that ran between realities was no more an obstacle to the feathered couriers than a fence between neighboring yards.

Did old man Crandall's soul hitch a ride with a

crow? What about Patrick's? I remembered Pete talking about the latest regressions and how someone said that crows were "feasting like kings" on the dead in fields. Was that their reward for bringing souls over? An endless buffet of corpses?

Maybe the blurry figure in the photograph wasn't able to steal souls directly, and so instead was simply reaching out to mark which ones to take and to prime the body through glassification. Maybe the soul would separate from the body then and drift free, like a boat cut loose from its moorings.

Mrs. Crandall slowed to a stop at the end of our driveway. Mom said thanks and Dad told her if she ever needed anything, just to let him know. She promised she would, and then she drove off. I looked down at my good black shoes, scuffed now, just as Pete had predicted.

"What about Uncle Dean?" I asked. "He didn't get a proper funeral." I was ignoring the fact that he wouldn't have gotten a proper funeral anyway, since Pastor Nolan had only planned to say a few words, not deliver a full-fledged eulogy. There wasn't time for those anymore. Not here or anywhere else.

“We’ll have a moment of silence for him later,” said Dad, “and remember how he made us all laugh and smile.”

“And I’ll make shepherd’s pie when the power comes back on,” said Mom. “That was always his favorite.”

“I’d like that,” said Dad.

“Me too,” I added.

TWENTY-SEVEN

"Here we are," said Mom, putting her big glass casserole dish down on the dining room table, which she'd set with one extra placement in honor of Uncle Dean. We were also using the good utensils and had candles lit like we did on special occasions.

"Should we say grace?" she asked. That was also something we usually reserved for Christmas and Easter and Thanksgiving.

"What's the point?" asked Pete. "Everyone was praying at church and look what happened there." He was annoyed and had been since the moment we got home. He'd been told that it was a day for remembrance and that he could have his radio back tomorrow.

Dad glared. "You know, your mother went to a lot of trouble to make this nice meal for us. The least you could do is not try to ruin it."

"It's fine, Logan," Mom said. She'd been doing a lot better since we got home from church, mostly, I think, because she'd been busy preparing and cooking.

"The hell it is," Dad disagreed.

"I wasn't trying to ruin anything," Pete argued. "I was just saying—"

"You're always just saying something," Dad replied. "But someday, son, you're going to have to learn that it isn't always in your best interest to open your mouth. There are times in our lives when we just have to bite our tongues, regardless of how mad or frustrated we might feel. That's just the way it is. That's reality."

There was a moment of awkward silence, and then Dad put his hands together and bowed his head. "*I'll* say grace," he said, closing his eyes.

Mom quickly put her own hands together and followed his lead, but not Pete, and not me either. It wasn't that I didn't want to say grace but because I saw the way that my older brother had set his jaw and crossed his arms in defiance, almost daring Dad to look up at him again before starting, which I was certain he would, and then our nice meal truly would be ruined. There would be an argument, and Pete would get sent to our room. Mom and I would sit there quietly until it was over, and then we'd eat, with nobody saying anything, just chewing and swallowing and feeling sad that our one empty placement had turned into two. I could already see it so clearly that it seemed inevitable.

I guess nothing is, though.

Instead the power went out without Dad or Mom even realizing it. Dad parted his lips to begin the prayer but got no further. The only sound that escaped was a gasp of air, a sudden inhalation, followed by silence.

The change didn't start in one place and then spread out from there, as it had with old man Crandall. It was more like that chemistry experiment we did once in science class, mixing iodine and starch together in water. One instant the water is clear, and the next it's black, the transformation happening so fast that you could blink your eyes and miss it. I didn't blink, though, and I don't think that Pete did either.

Mom was still waiting for grace. Perhaps she hadn't heard the intake of breath, or maybe she had simply mistaken it as a sigh from Pete. It wasn't until a crow cawed once from outside, close by, possibly right up on our roof, that she finally opened her eyes and lifted her head. Dad was solid glass, through and through, polished as a showroom Cadillac. Obsidian. Mom's face went instantly pale.

"No! No! No!" she said, jumping up from her chair. "No, Logan, you can't! You promised!"

I thought she was going to slap him for a second, the way you might slap someone who had fallen into a trance, but then she stopped herself, maybe because she was afraid to touch him, or maybe because she realized it was too late. Dad was gone. It was just the three of us now and nothing was going to change that. I watched as her arms fell uselessly to her sides. She began to sob.

TWENTY-EIGHT

Darkness came and went as the glass plague intensified. No longer was Griever's Mill just on the periphery of things, experiencing the ongoing nightmare to a lesser degree than everywhere else. We now sat right at its epicenter. Or maybe it only seemed that way, since even during those moments of blue sky and sun that still appeared like bright islands amidst a black ocean, there was a different sort of darkness that never lifted.

I decided to start sleeping downstairs on the big

chair near the fireplace. I wanted to be close to Dad just in case he came back, or even in case he shattered. I didn't want Mom to be the first to find him like that. Though in truth that probably wouldn't have happened anyway; she was pretty much avoiding the dining room entirely.

She moved through the house like a ghost now, stuck in an endless loop that began at her bed and ended at the kitchen window, the only occasional deviation from those two points being the bathroom, where she would sometimes run the water for an hour at a time, perhaps to drown out the sound of her crying, or maybe to drown out the sound of everything else, which, curiously, no longer included the normally incessant chatter of house sparrows. I hadn't seen the ones that lived in our yard since Dad's departure.

"I don't understand," Mom had whispered at the window after noticing their absence. "I don't understand what's happening." The loss of her birds was just one more insult to add to the rest, one more stupid and unfair kick to the teeth.

I didn't understand it either, especially since the

chickadees and nuthatches and finches were still around. It was only Mom's sparrows that had left, even her special bird, the leucistic one with white wings. It didn't make sense, and Mom appeared to be taking it personally, as if the universe intended to steal from her every last thing that she loved.

I felt like telling her, *I'm still here and I'm not leaving*, but her sadness stood like a wall I could barely see over, let alone break through or climb. And besides, I was sad, too, and she was my mother; she should have been comforting me.

In his own way, Pete was gone, too, adrift in the static and whispers of his radio, seeking solace in the voice of a stranger instead of in the company of what remained of his family. Maybe that was partly my fault for not staying with him in our room, but I'm not sure it would have mattered. Occasionally he would come down and enter the dining room, but it was always with a certain wariness, as if Dad had become an imposter who might suddenly wake.

I guess I worried about that as well. Not so much that he'd be an imposter, but that he might not recognize me as his son, or even his own reflection in a mirror. Worse yet, he might be stuck that way forever.

The ones who'd come back were showing no signs at all of returning to normal. It was as though they'd been partially lobotomized, or had witnessed things so awful and unthinkable that something inside their minds had simply let go, snapping like low-weight fishing line.

I kept on following the news because I felt like I should, but little of it actually touched me. I understood that entire economies were collapsing, and that shipments of food and supplies and medicine had pretty much stopped all over the world. I knew that in many of the big cities, food riots and looting had led to fires that now burned out of control, forcing families onto the streets with only the clothes on their backs and whatever else they could carry. Loved ones who'd turned to glass were simply left behind, to explode in the heat. Millions had turned to glass globally, and perhaps a third of them had shattered since then. Thousands had come back, but none of them in any meaningful way. Regression continued to be the only way to communicate with them, and those communications continued to be as much a source of frustration as they were of answers. Even under hypnosis, few responded to questioning. Most of what we learned came from repetition, as the few who talked shared similar details that hinted at a common experience. They spoke of fire and lightning, of blood and death; with wide-eyed intensity, they whispered of trenches of mud and pools of acid, of bones piled higher than the eye could see. It all seemed to be adding up to some sort of war—an End Times sort of war.

I understood all this, but the magnitude of it seemed so far above me and so far away, so impossible. Never mind that the proof was right there in front of me, his head bowed and his hands clasped firmly together.

It took me a while, but I finally screwed up my courage enough to touch him. I needed to know if he truly was as cold as he looked. I placed the back of my hand to his forehead, the same way that he and Mom always checked my temperature when I got sick. Surprisingly, he wasn't cold at all; in fact, the warmth of the glass seemed to match that of my own skin. This was reassuring to me, for surely warmth must represent life and cold the opposite.

I stood there for a long moment like that, with my hand against his head, not really thinking or remembering anything in particular, just feeling the presence of him. As long as he remained in one piece, I told myself, there was hope.

TWENTY-NINE

"I'm drawing your favorite bird," I told Dad. I held my pad up so he could see it, even though, of course, he *couldn't* see it. Dad couldn't see anything anymore, at least not in this world.

Like Pete, Dad wasn't really into birds, but he did have a favorite: the black-capped chickadee. He liked the sounds they made in the mornings when he was leaving for work, the *chicka-chicka-chicka*s and the *dee-dee-dee*s. The friendly chatter made him smile. It made me smile, too, as did the memory of him pausing on the front step, his ear cocked to listen.

I put my pad back down and continued working. "I'll show it to you again when I'm finished," I said.

"I don't think he can hear you," Pete said from behind me.

I started a little, my pencil nearly piercing the page. I hadn't heard him come down.

"I know he can't," I replied. "So what?"

Pete shrugged. "Just saying."

I glowered at him. He didn't have his radio on his shoulder, which was unusual.

"Did your batteries die again?" I asked. He'd already turned the house over twice to find more, and would likely start searching our neighbors' houses next—the abandoned ones, that is.

He shook his head. "I thought you might want to talk," he said.

"About what?"

He shrugged again. "I don't know, just stuff. Are you sleeping okay down here?"

"I guess so," I said. I wasn't, though. Not at all.

Pete glanced over at the fireplace, where I'd already stacked some wood in preparation for tonight. I'd been thinking about our family camping trips, and how this would be the first summer we didn't go on one. I thought it might be nice to have a fire, even though we didn't need the heat. Maybe I could roast a marshmallow.

"Don't forget to open the damper if you have a fire later," Pete said.

"I know," I told him.

"Okay," he replied. "Is Mom lying down again?"

"She has a migraine," I said, which was the same thing I'd told Constable Sheery earlier when he called to check in on us. He already knew about Dad, and had let others know as well. A few stopped by to say how sorry they were, and one even brought us a big box of fresh vegetables and eggs from his farm.

"Thought you could use this," he'd said. "Your dad helped my boy a couple of winters back, after he fell through some ice."

I asked him how his boy was doing now.

"He's doing just fine," the man told me.

"Good," I said. "Thanks."

"My wife is doing some canning," the man continued. "Maybe I'll come back again with some jars."

I said thanks again and waved at him as he drove

off, and that would be the last I ever saw of him. Perhaps he turned to glass like Dad did, or possibly his wife turned first, or maybe he just simply changed his mind, deciding that it wasn't worth burning all that gas, and that the canned food was too precious to part with. Whatever the case, I was glad to have what he'd already given us.

I had put the box down on the table close to Dad, but Pete had since moved it into the kitchen. I guess he didn't want to be reminded of our situation every time he felt like having a carrot.

Pete plopped himself down on the arm of the couch and glanced out between the open curtains. He started swinging his leg back and forth, and seemed sort of distracted and fidgety, like he was no longer sure what to do with himself if he didn't have a mostly dead speaker hissing into his ear.

"There's a woman in Mississippi who got arrested for shattering her husband with an ice pick," he finally said. "Her neighbor saw her do it, but they're not sure if they can charge her with murder since her husband wasn't technically alive anymore."

"He wasn't technically dead either," I pointed out. He probably wasn't even cold. Not if Dad was any indication.

"I know," said Pete. "That's the problem. What do you call it? Attempted murder? Manslaughter? Vandalism?"

"Why'd she do it?" I asked.

"She said he was abusive, and was scared that if he came back it might get worse. She showed the police some bruises."

"Self-defense?" I wondered.

Pete nodded. "That's what I said."

I thought about it a moment longer before deciding that it was probably a little more complicated than that. "Maybe she just didn't want to take care of him if he did come back," I said.

Dad used to warn us about only seeing things in black or white. He said the world was mostly shades of gray.

"Could you blame her if she didn't?" said Pete.

I shook my head. "I guess not, but she could've just left. There was no need to shatter him."

"I suppose," said Pete, although it was clear by the

look on his face that he didn't think the woman had done anything wrong. I started to wonder how many others around the world had been shattered on purpose. In the absence of any witnesses, how would anyone know? You could just pretend that it was spontaneous fragmentation and people would pretty much have to believe you.

I shuddered to think of how people like the Messam twins might react to this realization. By going on shattering sprees, perhaps—turning their slingshots on their neighbors instead of using them to break old windows in abandoned buildings. I wondered if we should keep our curtains closed just in case Lars came sniffing around.

It occurred to me then as I thought of the twins that Pete and I had never gone back to get our wagon. Had anyone found it there in the alley? Did it even matter?

Pete stopped swinging his leg and stood up. "I'm gonna go check on Mom," he said.

I noticed belatedly that he had tucked in his shirt, and tried to remember if this was the first time he'd ever done so. I was pretty sure it was, and I almost asked him why, but then I noticed that he was also wearing one of Dad's belts, and it hit me. With Dad being gone, Pete now considered himself to be the man of the house.

I felt a sudden rush of anger, and it must have shown in my eyes, as Pete paused before going upstairs.

"What?" he asked.

"That's Dad's belt."

He looked down at the belt and then back up at me. "So?"

"So, he didn't tell you that you could wear it."

"Well, I can't exactly ask him, can I?"

"Take it off," I said.

He gave me a weird look.

"And since when do you tuck in your shirt?" I asked him.

"What difference does it make?"

"Dad didn't leave you in charge," I reminded him. "He told us to look after each other."

"I'm the oldest," Pete said flatly.

"Barely."

"Still," he said. "I am." And then he turned and left the room, saying, "I'll be upstairs if you need me," over his shoulder.

I don't need you! I almost yelled at him, but the words never got past my lips, because they weren't true. I needed him as my brother and as my friend, just as I needed Mom to be my mom again. I looked down at my half-finished chickadee and started to cry.

THIRTY

I awoke at four a.m. to a noise outside. It sounded like gasping and heaving, like someone in the process of being sick.

I sat up, forgetting for a moment that I was on the living room chair and not in my bed. I glanced sideways at the fireplace, where a few small embers continued to glow. Then I cocked my head and listened, wondering if maybe I'd dreamed the sound.

Nope, there it was again, definitely coming from outside, and close, too.

I crept to the window and pulled the corner of the

curtain just a fraction of an inch away from the wall so I could look out without being seen by anyone who might be looking in. A drunk, perhaps, throwing up out there in our grass. Or maybe not. The front yard was empty, so I pulled the curtain back just a little bit farther. I could now see the driveway as well, and sure enough there was somebody there, crouched low beside the back tire of Dad's truck.

My heart started pounding. I squinted to see better, and noticed that the person was holding a hose that ran down from the truck's gas tank to a jerry can on the driveway. The person hunched over sideways and retched again, and immediately I understood what had happened: He must have swallowed some of the gas when he started siphoning. I'd seen Uncle Dean siphon once from a wrecked car in his garage and I knew that if you weren't careful doing it, things could go badly.

I stood there watching for a minute, not really sure what to do. I couldn't just let someone take our gas, could I? It seemed cowardly not to do something, but what? Knock on the window to let him know I could see him? Go outside and try to chase him off? What if I wasn't able to? What if the person got violent? Uncle

Dean's truck was still out there, too, so it wasn't as if we didn't have a vehicle with fuel.

I was still debating with myself when the person pulled the hose out and rotated the gas cap back on again. He stood up then, his body now partially silhouetted by the streetlight, or rather, *her* body. The shape and curves left no question that this was a woman.

She paused before making off with our fuel, looking this way and that to make sure that no one had seen her, the light from the streetlamp hitting her face just long enough for me to recognize her. It was Mrs. Gilmour from the end of the block—a nice woman who taught piano and who had babysat Pete and me a few times when we were younger. I remembered that she'd baked us cookies. Peanut butter cookies.

I wasn't sure why, but this realization made me pull the curtain all the way to the side.

The movement must have registered in Mrs. Gilmour's periphery, because she immediately turned and looked right at me, then shrank like a thief caught red-handed, which I guess she was. Her expression was lost in shadow now, but I imagined that if I could see it, I would find shame there, and desperation, and perhaps even a touch of defensiveness, since she must've needed the gas real bad or she wouldn't be stealing it.

A moment passed as we considered each other. I finally lifted my hand and waved at her, just a simple hello in the dead of the night, between neighbors. She waved back, and then quietly went on her way, her gas can firmly in hand. I closed the curtain and returned to my chair.

THIRTY-ONE

A week went by, most of it passing in darkness. I started to wonder how people could live in the Arctic Circle with no sun for months at a time. I wondered how they stayed sane.

The meat in our freezer all spoiled. The electricity wasn't coming on often enough, or staying on long enough, to keep it frozen. Pete said the outages were due to some kind of interference, sort of like how the power grid could go down when particles from the sun interfered with the atmosphere. In that case you'd at least have some pretty northern lights to look at.

I assumed that Pete had gotten this from his radio. Whether or not it was true hardly seemed to matter. I'd pretty much given up on the news myself.

Mom was trying. Or at least she was trying to try. She made a point of getting up in the morning to make us breakfast, but after that her momentum always stalled, and by two in the afternoon she'd have a headache and be curled up in bed with the lights off (whether we had electricity or not).

"I'm gonna go lie down for a while now," she'd always tell us. "Please don't leave the house." Her skin was pale and she seemed to be getting shakier by the day. Was she sick but not letting on? I looked for the lemon ginger tea that she liked to drink with honey whenever she was feeling under the weather, but I couldn't find any. Maybe we were out. It had been a while since the last time we stopped by Mom's favorite tea shop.

Pete took it upon himself to decide what we should eat for lunches and suppers, as if someone had appointed him Chief of Rationing or something. He got mad at me once when I tried to eat some canned peaches.

"We have to save all the canned food for later," he

told me. "Have some crackers instead. There's some Ritz on the lazy Susan."

"I don't *want* crackers," I argued. "And besides, I know you had some pineapple the other night. I found the can in the garbage." I could've also mentioned that I was the only one who was actually bothering to even take the garbage out—not that anyone had come to pick any of it up.

"I skipped supper that night," Pete said defensively. "Plus, I'm the only one here who even *likes* pineapple!"

"That's not the point."

"Whatever," Pete went on. "I just think we need to be smarter about what we eat now and what we save for later."

"Fine," I said. "I won't eat any canned peaches."

"And I won't eat any more pineapple," he agreed.

Dad could shatter at any moment and there we were arguing about canned fruit. It was ridiculous. *Beyond* ridiculous. We were eleven and twelve years old; we shouldn't have had to worry about any of the stuff that was happening. We should have been out on our bikes or setting off firecrackers; we should have been gluing together model airplanes or doing cannonballs at the pool. At the very least, I should have been outside birding with Mom. The glass plague had ruined everything, which I guess was why I felt a faint glimmer of hope when Pete finally mentioned a plan.

"What plan?" I asked him. He had come down into the basement to find me. I was sitting in the room that Uncle Dean had been sleeping in, and was in the process of adding another species to my drawing pad, a brown creeper this time. The room had no windows, so if I turned off the switch and just drew by candlelight, I would never have to know if the sky turned ugly and the power went off.

"A plan to end the glass plague," said Pete. "For good." His face looked orange in the candlelight. His eyes were dark shadows.

I wanted to believe him, but the fact that he didn't seem hopeful or excited at all made me suspicious.

"How?"

He didn't lay it out right away. "It's just an idea right now, and it's sorta controversial."

I narrowed my eyes, not understanding how an end to one of the worst things in human history could possibly be controversial.

"What is it?" I asked.

"You won't like it."

"Just tell me!"

He looked at me for a long moment, the small candle flames now bouncing in time with my heart, as if my anticipation had somehow manifested itself in fire. "All right," he finally said. "I'll tell you." And then he did.

I didn't get mad or freak out, although I definitely should have. I guess the shock of it was just too much for me. I kept thinking that Pete must have gotten it wrong, that he must have misunderstood or misinterpreted whatever he'd heard. That, or it was a joke.

"Shatter them *ourselves*?" I finally said. "On purpose? *That's* the plan?"

"The voice says that desperate times call for desperate measures," Pete replied.

I stared at him, wondering when "the guy on the radio" had become "the Voice," as if his was the only one that mattered. And Pete hadn't criticized the plan at all. Was it possible that he actually agreed with it? I couldn't bring myself to ask him straight-out, so instead I simply whispered, "We can't, Pete. He's our dad."

"He *was* our dad," he replied, his expression as hard as forged iron. "He's something else now…."

THIRTY-TWO

Pete explained it to me like the radio had explained it to him: There was a war being waged between darkness and light, between good and evil. It was probably the Big War, the Final War, and it wasn't going the way that it was supposed to. Normally the devil relied on the souls of the damned to give life to his demon soldiers, but not anymore. Through glassification, the souls of the living and unjudged could now be conscripted as well, or maybe *harvested* was a better word. Clearly that's what it was—not a plague, as everyone had been saying, but a harvest.

The glass storms that swept through our skies were like short-lived conduits for the devil's dark will, briefly potent but unsustainable, at least for now. The process of glassification itself was a bit of a mystery, but it was believed that it was achieved through the use of dark matter, and that its purpose was to create a state of being in which the body was neither alive nor dead, but in a sort of stasis that the soul couldn't fully cling to, leaving it vulnerable.

Those who were taken were slaves now. As for the ones who'd returned, it was said that the process wasn't perfect, and that the dark matter used to make proxies wasn't always stable. When it failed, the soul was split, with half of it remaining on the other side and half returning to this one, like what had happened with old man Crandall, who could never be made whole again. And those who had shattered could never be brought back to life. If you died on that side, you died on this one, and vice versa.

All this, Pete informed me, was the "Unified Theory of Glassification," which I thought was basically just a fancy way of saying "Our Best Guess." The people doing the guessing were scientists and academics and scholars, and whoever the voice on the radio belonged to (nobody seemed to know).

"If we shatter them all at once," Pete finally concluded, "then the devil will lose all those soldiers at the same time. Think of how vulnerable he'd be. God could win."

"But it would be murder," I said at length, still shocked at the sheer audacity of it.

Pete shook his head. "It's not that simple, Ben."

"Of course it is!"

Pete sighed. "We at least have to think about it."

I couldn't believe he was serious. I struggled to find any words.

"Nothing's for sure yet," Pete continued. "Right now it's just an idea."

"It's a stupid idea," I said. "If the devil can take our souls, then God can, too. I bet he'll start to, just to make things even."

Pete was shaking his head before I even finished, as if this scenario had already been measured and weighed and discarded.

"He can't," he told me. "He'd be taking our free will if he did. And somehow I doubt that he's going to show up to ask for volunteers. It's up to us, Ben. We have to stop it on our own."

"Not like this," I said.

"It might be the only way."

I stared at the candle flame for a moment, digging my fingernails into my palms.

"No," I finally said. "I won't do it, and I won't let you do it either. I'll tell Mom. She'll probably ground you to your room just for talking about it."

"She already knows," Pete informed me. "I told her this morning."

I remembered then that Pete had gone in to check on her after lunch. He'd been in there for a while, too.

"What'd she say?" I asked him. "That you were crazy?"

"She didn't say anything, just laid there staring off into nowhere. Something's wrong with her, Ben. Really wrong. She's worse than I've ever seen her."

"And how do you think she'll be if you shatter Dad? You'd pretty much be killing her, too."

"Nothing's for sure yet," he said again. "It's not like there's been a date set for the shattering."

The Shattering. It was like the name of a horror

movie. I almost said it out loud just to hear how it sounded, only I couldn't quite force the words past my lips. To name a thing, some inner voice told me, was to give it power, and the last thing I wanted to do was give power to madness. Surely that's what this was. It had to be.

THIRTY-THREE

There was whiskey in the cupboard above the fridge. That's where Dad kept it, I knew. I also knew that sometimes, after a particularly stressful day, he would take the bottle out and pour a little in a glass, over ice. It seemed to help, and I'd always wondered why. I had also always wondered what it tasted like, and why some people liked to get drunk and other people didn't, why it made some of them laugh and talk loudly (like Uncle Dean), while others just got mean and angry (like James Messam). It seemed strange that the exact same substance could have such different effects on different people.

Most people don't know it, but there are birds that get drunk, too. They don't really do it on purpose, but it isn't exactly by accident either.

The birds I mean are called Bohemian waxwings. They're about the same size as starlings and have orange-and-black heads and beautiful yellow-and-red-tipped wings. They live up north in the boreal forest—away from us humans and all our crazy problems—but in the cold months, when the forest insects they usually feed on are gone, they move south in massive flocks in search of berries, which they gorge themselves on until spring.

Waxwings are tough birds. They don't fly as far south as most birds do, so they have to put up with snow and frigid temperatures. The berries they eat are often frozen solid, and they have to eat a lot of them to fuel their energy needs. I read once that a single waxwing can sometimes eat its own weight in berries in a single day. A hungry flock of them can strip a whole tree in a day or two.

They do this all winter long, moving from one area to another, sometimes in small flocks of just a few dozen, but often in flocks of thousands, and they don't all eat together at the same time; for every bird that's gulping down berries, there's another perched high in the tree on the lookout for predators like merlins or sharp-shinned hawks. The birds take turns, constantly switching places with one another. Sometimes they even feed each other, offering their freshly plucked berries to their nearest neighbor. Waxwings are always looking out for each other. It's one of the reasons they're my favorite birds.

Waxwings usually don't head north again until April, which means that they're still around when the snow starts melting and the temperature rises. That's when the berries thaw and the sugar inside them causes them to ferment right there on the trees, basically turning them into alcoholic berries. The waxwings continue to eat them, and if they end up eating too many, they'll actually get sloshed.

You can sometimes tell that the birds are drunk by the way they're flying. They'll almost run into you if you're standing right in their flight path. There was one time that I had several hundred of them flying past me and around me from one tree to another, coming so close that I had to tuck my arms in tight to my sides in order not to be grazed by their beautiful wings as they passed me.

You'd think it would be comical, seeing so many

drunk birds like that, and in a way I guess it was, but all I can remember thinking at the time was how amazing it was, being surrounded by all that chaotic motion, that swirling vortex of color and sound. It made me feel like I was a part of something special, something wild and wonderfully free. I closed my eyes and experienced a lightness, as if I were floating above the snow instead of standing in it, as if the whirlwind of wings had lifted me right off my feet and swept me up into the heart of the flock. Where I belonged, I remembered thinking, strangely.

I certainly never felt like I belonged at school, where hardly anyone ever looked out for anyone else, where a bully could be barreling right toward you across the playground and no one would offer so much as a peep of warning. Instead they would simply stand there, breathing a sigh of relief that the bully's attention wasn't on them. I guess that's just how humans are. Maybe not all of us, and not all the time, but most of us, and often.

I saw the waxwings many times that winter and early spring, from the growing warmth of early April all the way back to the frigid mornings at the start of January, some of them so brutally windy and bitterly cold that I was certain no bird in existence could possibly survive outside.

We always think of birds as being such small and breakable things, all soft feathers and no weight at all, wings of little more substance than toothpicks and parchment paper, and yet when we humans are balled up under blankets in front of the fireplace, they're out there in the harsh world enduring it all, and not only that, but they're singing.

Maybe *we're* the breakable things, fragile in heart and mind, souls as wispy and weak as a single tissue. Maybe someday when we're all gone and the birds are still around, they'll think to sing a song in our memory, just a few flat notes to mark our passing. Maybe that's all we're worth.

I carried a chair from the dining room into the kitchen. It was the only way that I could reach to get Dad's whiskey.

THIRTY-FOUR

I awoke with the left side of my face feeling wet against a cushion. When I sat up, I realized why; I'd puked there, and then passed out in it. It wasn't a lot of puke, but still. I could smell it, and it stank like the whiskey. I shuddered, and then stood up, feeling a little wobbly.

I went to the kitchen and cleaned myself off, passing Dad on my way, and feeling guilty for what I'd done. I imagined him shaking his head at me, his eyes full of disappointment.

The house was quiet. Mom had apparently not come

down to make us breakfast today. I quickly looked in on her before brushing my teeth to get rid of the pasty alcohol taste. She was sleeping.

I went back downstairs. The air in the house seemed thick and stale, and felt heavy inside my lungs. I opened a window, but it wasn't enough.

I need to get outside, I thought. *I need fresh air.* But first I needed some water. I drank down two full glasses, filling myself with liquid since I couldn't stomach the thought of food.

I got my shoes on and went out onto the front step, thinking that I would just sit there for a while, hungover like some old hobo. Only I didn't. The compulsion to get outside quickly turned into a compulsion to leave, to get away from my house and my family and everything else, if only just for a while.

I started walking, but not with any particular destination in mind. It was partly cloudy, the wind blowing just hard enough to rustle leaves. I turned left at the end of the street, and then right at the end of that one, and soon I was on my way somewhere, my feet having apparently decided this for me.

Sometimes, on Sunday afternoons after church, Mom would let me come with her to a tiny tea shop on the corner of First Street. We would walk there, taking our time and pointing out birds along the way, occasionally stopping for a moment or two just to listen, which probably looked strange to those passing by, a mother and son standing totally motionless on the edge of the sidewalk, heads cocked off to the side. All we needed was a matching pair of tinfoil hats.

The tea shop was called Holga's Herbal Happiness, and Mom loved going there. She said it was like taking an olfactory vacation. From mint leaves and orange blossoms to ginger root and lemon, the shop housed the smells of more teas than I would have believed even existed. Admittedly, though, my own reasons for tagging along had less to do with my nose than they did with my fondness for black licorice.

Holga kept a jar of licorice under her counter, but not the twisty packaged kind like at the corner store. This was authentic licorice, the pieces small and round and much too salty to even qualify as candy. Eating it made you wince. It cleared your sinuses and made your eyes water, but for some reason I craved it. Holga told me one time that she and I were the only two people in town who were brave enough to eat the stuff.

Mom tried it once and almost gagged, and afterward demanded a free cuppa (as Holga called it) to wash the foul taste out of her mouth. Holga already had a kettle on, so in short order they were both sipping honey-sweetened chamomile and gossiping.

I tried not to listen in, focusing instead on the taste of my licorice and whatever was happening outside the window at the front of the shop, where a hummingbird feeder hung from a tree. I had never actually seen a hummingbird drink from it, but maybe someday I would.

I wondered sometimes, while Mom and Holga went on about books or gardening, what Pete and Dad were talking about. I'd always assumed that while I was spending time with Mom, Pete and Dad must have been hanging out together, too, probably discussing muscle cars and football with Uncle Dean. I imagined them at the garage, laughing at dirty jokes and drinking 7UPs from the vending machine.

I assumed all this, but when I finally got around to actually asking, Pete just gave me a funny look.

"What do you mean?" he asked me.

"On Sunday, when I'm at the tea shop with Mom," I repeated. "Where do you and Dad go? What do you guys talk about?"

"We don't go anywhere," Pete replied. "We don't talk about anything. We just come home." There was bitterness in his voice. He tried to hide it but failed. I could hear the hurt, too.

"Oh." I should have left it at that, but I didn't. "You guys must at least watch sports together."

"Why does it even matter?" Pete asked, his wounded pride turning to anger.

I shrugged. "It doesn't, I guess. I just assumed..."

"Don't you have anything better to do than bug me with stupid questions? Maybe you should go drink tea and listen to some birds. I swear sometimes that I have a sister instead of a brother."

I kept on walking, thinking about Mom the whole way. I was hoping that maybe Holga might come over if I asked her to. Maybe a friend could get through to Mom in a way that Pete and I couldn't. At the very least, I could bring home some tea, and maybe the smell of it throughout the house, and the warmth of it in her stomach, would make Mom feel better. If I could get her to smile just once, I thought, then maybe I could find other ways to reach her, and little by little, day by day, the person she used to be would start to take over from the ghost she'd become. Hopefully before Pete did something crazy.

It was seven blocks from our house to Holga's. I took a shortcut through the park and got there in under fifteen minutes, only to discover that not only was Holga not there, but the tea shop was completely shut up, the windows all boarded over with plywood. The sign above the door was gone, too, but you could still see the outline of all the letters on account of the sun having faded the surrounding wood.

I sighed and stood there for a moment, staring. The whole block was eerily silent. I looked left past Leroy's skate and bike shop, and then right past the laundromat and the old arcade (which mostly just had pinball machines now). The sidewalks were empty, and for a moment I imagined myself the lone occupant of some evacuated outpost in the middle of nowhere. I could scream if I wanted to and no one would hear me. I could shatter glass and kick in doorways and no one would care.

Had Holga left anything behind? Was the stockroom still full of tea? I decided to find out, but first I needed something to help me pry off the plywood.

A search through a bin in the alley yielded a broken tripod leg. After screwing off its rubber foot, I managed to jam the metal end of it in behind the wood covering the back basement window. I felt bad for breaking in, but Mom needed a jolt and I was desperate.

It took all my weight as leverage, but finally the nails gave way with an audible groan. I tossed the plywood off to the side and then set about breaking the glass as quietly as possible. My heart was pounding but I tried to stay calm as I cleared away all the fragments. It was an awkward seven-foot drop to the basement floor, but I managed it okay.

Thankfully, the power was on and the light switches worked.

I was in the larger of two separate storerooms, both of which were empty save for a few bare shelves and a small stack of collapsed boxes. I went up the short stairwell to the main part of the store, already knowing what I'd find there (nothing), but still foolishly holding out hope for something different.

Although some of the old scents still lingered, nothing remained of the tea stock. The room had been gutted completely except for Holga's old counter, which was probably screwed down into the floor. I sighed, saddened now as well as disappointed.

Since the counter was still there, I decided to look behind it. Unlikely as it seemed, I was hoping that the black licorice at least might have been forgotten. It wasn't, of course, but the glass jar itself was actually there, sitting like an empty reminder. I sighed again. That's when I heard a sound from the opposite side of the shop.

I looked up to see Lars Messam standing in the doorway to the storeroom, blocking my only way out. Worse yet, he was holding the metal tripod leg that I'd used to pry my way inside. He smiled at me, showing teeth.

THIRTY-FIVE

Well, well, well," Lars said, still smiling. "Looks like poor little Benji has backed himself into a corner." He laughed maniacally.

The Messams always called me Benji, after that small dog from the movies we always watched at school when *Finding Nemo* was already checked out and my teacher was too tired to teach. They had nicknames for almost everyone they terrorized, most of them having something to do with animals. Now that I knew what they did for fun in their backyard, in their sandbox-turned-firepit, I understood why.

My skin went instantly cold. It didn't matter that Lars was alone and only half the threat that he normally would have been. I knew I was in more danger now than I'd ever been inside my school or out on the playground. The tea shop was closed and boarded up, and nobody knew I was there. Lars could do anything he felt like and no one would see or hear.

"What do you want?" I asked, trying and failing to keep my voice calm. I was pretty sure he wouldn't go so far as to kill me, but it was easy enough to imagine him leaving me there on the floor with a broken leg. What would I do then? How would I get out?

"I want you to whimper," he told me. "Whimper like the scared little runt you are." He started making dog sounds, a series of sad whines and howls, eerie in their authenticity.

"Just let me go!" I begged him. "I can give you stuff. I've got hockey cards and comic books. They're yours. You can have them."

"I don't want your stupid cards and comics," he told me. "I want you to scream like my brother screamed." He took a few steps toward me, smacking his open palm with the end of the tripod leg. He shook his head. "You shouldn't have left your wagon behind. You probably thought it wouldn't matter, that I wouldn't recognize it from when you and your dimwit brother delivered flyers, but I did."

"It's not my fault that Lester stepped in the trap," I said.

"You were trespassing. If you hadn't been, it wouldn't have happened. Lester would still be here instead of lying in a stupid hospital bed in Paulson. That's your fault." He pointed an accusatory finger and continued his slow approach.

Panic was setting in now, heightened by a sudden feeling that not only was Lars getting nearer, but that the walls were closing in, too. The whole room was shrinking around me. Escape was impossible. My only option was to stand and fight.

I took a deep breath and clenched my fists, preparing for the inevitable.

It was then that a second figure appeared at the storeroom entrance. My first thought was that Lars hadn't come alone. I imagined his father, probably drunk and hungry for revenge, but my brain was working faster than my eyes. It wasn't old man Messam at all. It was Pete, holding what appeared to be a fish bat, probably the same one I'd seen him club rainbow trout with on numerous occasions.

"Hey, jerk-face!" Pete yelled. "Leave my little brother alone!"

I should have been grateful for his sudden arrival, I should have felt glad that I didn't have to face Lars all on my own, but instead I felt a pang of resentment. It came from those two simple words and how they sounded when Pete put them together: *little brother*, as if I were six instead of eleven, as if I were completely incapable of taking care of myself even though I'd been doing exactly that for nearly two weeks now.

Lars had jumped at the unexpected sound of Pete's voice, but was quick to regain his composure. He turned to Pete and then back to me, his body sideways so that he could keep us both in view. If he ever stopped smiling, it was too brief for me to notice.

"All right," he said. "Which one of you two monkeys wants to go first?"

Despite the fact that it was two on one now, he actually seemed to be looking forward to it.

The corner of the counter stood between Lars and

me, so my right hand was out of sight. I closed my fingers around the empty jar. It was the same kind of jar that Mom used for canning, the glass thick and heavy. I picked it up, my heart now pounding like crazy.

Lars was two-handing the broken tripod leg like a baseball bat, and would likely knock the jar right out of the air if my timing wasn't just right. What I needed was for Pete to command all his attention for at least a second or two.

Those two words kept going through my mind: *little brother, little brother.* Lars was a little brother, too, it occurred to me. Only by a few minutes, but with Lester as a sibling, that wouldn't matter. I'd seen how the two of them were in the schoolyard, the way Lester always chose the target and just expected Lars to follow along, which he did without fail. *Little brother* probably meant the same thing to Lars that it did to me. He probably carried the same resentments that I did. The only question was, could I use this against him? I decided to make that gamble.

I gritted my teeth and looked at Pete. "Get lost!" I told him. "I didn't ask for your help and I don't want it. Just go away."

It was hard to tell who was more surprised by my words, Lars or Pete. They both stared at me in disbelief, although on Pete's face there was also hurt. He'd appeared like a hero at just the right moment, only to be told to bug off by the very person who needed rescuing. And as for Lars, it was clear by the look on his face that he himself would never have dared to talk to Lester like I was now talking to Pete.

His attention quickly shifted away from me and settled on Pete. How would big brother react? He was obviously dying to know.

I brought my jar up and reared back to throw it, only I hadn't considered one thing: After what I'd just said, Pete wasn't sure if the jar was meant for Lars or for him. His eyes widened, which was all the clue that Lars needed. He turned back toward me just in time to see the glass missile flying toward his head.

He managed to duck away from it while at the same time springing toward me, his anger bolstered by what I had just attempted to do to him. His arm came up, and then the world went black. I came to a moment later on the floor, my head ringing and my eyes seeing stars.

The broken tripod leg was beside me on the floor,

too, I realized, and Pete was standing over it, yelling, "Bug off or I'll give you another one!"

I sat up, the world spinning.

"You're gonna pay for that!" growled Lars. He was on the opposite side of the room now and holding his arm in a way that made it obvious Pete had landed a pretty good shot with his trusty fish bat, probably while Lars was preoccupied with me.

I blinked my eyes a few times just to make sure that I wasn't hallucinating. Had Pete really done what we'd so often dreamed of and actually turned the tables on a Messam? It sure looked that way, though I wasn't confident that Lars was quite finished yet. He gritted his teeth and flexed his arm as if testing whether he could still use it. I could tell by the look on his face that the effort pained him, but somehow he still managed to turn the grimace into a smile.

"Stay back!" Pete warned him again.

Lars stood his ground and flexed his arm a second time. "Hits a man with his back turned and now he thinks he's a tough guy."

"You're not a man," said Pete. "And if you touch *my* brother again, you'll be joining *yours* in the hospital."

He was talking big, but it was obvious that he was still afraid, and fear was what the Messam twins fed on. Fear was their everything.

"We'll see about that," said Lars, a murderous glint in his eyes. "We'll just see."

Sensing that round two might be imminent and that Pete might not get so lucky twice, I grabbed the broken tripod leg and unsteadily got to my feet beside my brother, who I wasn't any less angry at but was at least willing to work with for the next few minutes.

"Dumb and dumber, side by side," said Lars, but words were all he had now. As scared as Pete and I might still be, we both had weapons. Lars was unarmed and outnumbered, and a little bit injured as well. A reluctant retreat was really his only option. It took a moment, but he seemed to come to this realization as well. He slowly backed up toward the stairs, all the while shaking his head and wagging his finger at us, as if to say, *Next time, next time...*

And then he was gone.

THIRTY-SIX

If Pete expected a thank-you, he wasn't going to get one. As soon as I got outside and determined that Lars wasn't out there waiting for us, I walked off and left Pete behind me, or at least I tried to. He quickly caught up, his radio firmly in hand. He must have brought it with him and set it down outside the tea shop's window before following me in, or rather, before following Lars in.

I could only assume that Pete had been tailing me from a distance since I left the house, and that Lars had somehow managed to get between us. I guess I should have been watching for Lars when I passed the arcade.

He and Lester always used to hang out there, scaring quarters out of all the kids.

I started walking faster.

"Hey, wait up!" Pete told me.

"Just leave me alone," I said. My head was pounding. I reached up to feel where I'd taken the hit.

"What's your problem?" he asked me. "I just saved your sorry butt, in case you hadn't noticed. What the heck were you doing in there anyway?"

"Doesn't matter. You'd just say that it was stupid."

I changed direction and kept on going.

"C'mon, Ben. Don't be like that. We need to get home and put some ice on that eye before it swells shut."

"We don't *have* any ice," I reminded him. "It all *melted*." If Pete hadn't been so busy listening to his radio, he might have noticed.

"Fine, forget the ice, then. We still need to get home. Mom's probably worried sick."

"I bet she hasn't even noticed," I said, which was probably a little unfair, for as much as she'd been walking around the house like a zombie, I knew that she still cared. It was obvious that Pete did, too, or he wouldn't have come after me, but I wasn't about to acknowledge that. I kept walking north, the complete opposite direction of home.

"Fine," said Pete. "Just keep walking, then. I'll go home by myself. I'll be the responsible one."

I turned and charged him then, the rage that I had hoped to release on Lars Messam coming out belatedly. I didn't go for Pete—I went for his radio. Only I wasn't quick enough. Between the residual effects of a hangover and the more immediate effects of having my bell rung, my balance and reflexes weren't what they should have been.

Pete deftly swung the radio away from me and spun around as I passed, like a matador gracefully avoiding a bull.

I would have tried a second charge, but I somehow got my legs crossed while turning and ended up tripping over my own two feet. I reached out to brace for impact, scraping both of my palms on the sidewalk. I had to scream then, not out of pain or anger, but out of frustration.

Pete looked down at me like I was having some sort of meltdown, which I guess I was. I sat on the curb, looking at my burning palms and feeling the beat of my heart in the angry lump just above my eye. All this for some licorice and tea.

"Now can we go home?" Pete asked me. "Please?"

I sighed and got to my feet, and twenty minutes later we were tromping through our front door, into the same stale air that I'd left behind, although it was a little bit better because of the window I'd left open.

Mom wasn't there to greet us as we came in. She didn't run up to hug us and tell us how worried she had been, or how close she had come to calling Wayne Sheery. She didn't inspect my wound with a careful finger, or go to the bathroom to get the gauze and the hydrogen peroxide. I'd been right when I said that she probably hadn't even noticed that we were gone. She was still curled up in bed when we looked in on her, in exactly the same position as she'd been before.

Pete and I shared a worried look, after which I went into the bathroom to take care of my injuries on my own. I opened the medicine cabinet, and that's when I noticed the pills—Mom's pills. The bottle that Dad and I picked up in Paulson was completely full. Mom hadn't been taking them.

THIRTY-SEVEN

My eye continued to swell to the point that I could barely open it by the next day. But at least my headache was gone.

As always, the first thing I did upon waking was look over at Dad, to make sure that he was still there, which he was, although he wasn't alone. Mom was sitting with him at the dining room table.

At first I thought this might be a positive development, that Mom might finally be facing what had happened, but as I got closer to the table, the reality became clear.

Mom was drinking cold instant coffee that she obviously hadn't stirred real well. There were coffee grounds on both the lip of the mug and at the corners of her mouth. She didn't seem to notice. Her eyes held an eerie intensity.

"I should have known," she said, mostly to herself. "I should have guessed." She was more alert than I'd seen her in weeks, but not in a good way.

"Guessed what?" I asked her, while reminding myself that today I would have to make sure that she took her pill.

"My sparrows," Mom said. "The merlin must have killed them."

Merlins are small brown falcons that often feed on songbirds. There was one that had been nesting in our neighborhood for years. She usually used the same tree, a tall pine that was just five doors down from our place. I didn't often see her, but regularly heard the loud keening sound that she made to attract a mate, which this year she hadn't, so far as I could tell. Normally her offspring would have fledged by this point in the summer, but I'd only seen or heard just her.

"I don't think so, Mom," I said. As efficient as

merlins were at hunting sparrows, there was no way that only one of them could have devastated a whole flock so quickly. Besides, it was dragonfly season, and the falcon was most likely feasting on big flying bugs.

"Yes," Mom went on, nodding to herself, and not even acknowledging the fact that I'd spoken. "Had to be. It's the only thing that makes sense." She sucked back the rest of her coffee in one mad gulp, spilling some in the process. A dark rivulet ran down her chin.

"She's a menace," Mom continued, looking right through me, like I wasn't even there. "She has to be stopped. None of the songbirds are safe. She'll pick them all off one by one, until there's nothing left but glass."

"Glass?" I said, getting very worried now. "Mom, are you okay?"

"Something has to be done," she said. She belatedly wiped her mouth and chin, leaving an ugly brown stain on the sleeve of an otherwise clean white shirt. "I wonder if there's gas in the chain saw...."

Given the state she was in, I wouldn't have trusted her with a letter opener, never mind a chain saw. She pushed herself up from her chair, her eyes sweeping past Dad as if he'd become just another piece of furniture in the room.

I got up to follow her. "Just wait a sec, Mom. Hold on. It couldn't have been the merlin. It had to be something else. Just stop and think about it."

But she was beyond logic or common sense. She was operating on impulse now, a slave to her own hysteria, and I had a horrible feeling that whatever spell she was under probably wasn't going to break until after she did whatever it was that she planned on doing. She put on her sandals and went out the back door.

I knew that I had to stop her, but first I ran to the stairwell and yelled, "Pete! Get down here! Mom needs us!" I listened for a second, but there was no answer. "Pete!" I yelled again. Still nothing. I swore and bolted up the stairs, throwing open the door to our room. It was empty. Where the heck was Pete? I went back downstairs and out the door, forgetting to even put my shoes on.

Mom had gone into the garage, and was already on her way out of it when I got outside. She had the chain saw in her hands, her face a resolute mask. It was obvious that she must have suffered some sort of mental break. I immediately moved to block her, my focus so fixed on the empty insanity in her eyes that I didn't see the rake on the ground by my feet. I stepped on the outermost prong, with only a sock to protect my foot.

An explosion of pain sent me hopping sideways. I screamed and fell to my knees, tears filling my eyes almost instantly. Mom walked right past me, her focused intensity more than a match for maternal instinct.

I gritted my teeth and forced myself to stand up, the pain searing. I didn't have to look to know that my foot was bleeding. I could already feel the wetness of it soaking into my sock. I limped forward, keeping the heel of my injured foot elevated as I went. I couldn't even see Mom anymore, but it was obvious where she was going, so I struggled along as best as I could, cursing myself for leaving my shoes behind.

By the time I finally made it out onto the street, Mom was already standing at the base of the merlin's nest tree. I looked up and, sure enough, the small falcon was there, perched like some bird-of-prey Christmas tree topper. It flew off, keening, as the high-revving growl of the chain saw tore a hole in the silence of the morning.

“Mom!” I yelled, adrenaline now numbing my foot, allowing me to actually run.

The lowermost branches were gone in an instant, clearing the way for Mom to attack the trunk itself. A few of our neighbors had come out onto their steps, but they all remained there, obviously wary of the crazy woman with the chain saw.

I yelled again as the spinning chain bit deep into wood. The sound was high and horrible and seemed to go on forever. Mom managed to cut a perfect sideways V into the trunk, allowing the tree to fall lengthways along the sidewalk instead of on our neighbors’ cars or houses.

I whispered, “Timber,” as Mom stepped clear, and with a groan like a rumble from deep in the belly of a hungry whale, followed by one loud crack and a rapid series of smaller snaps, the huge pine settled in a massive green heap upon the ground.

Mom had hoped to scare off one bird, but instead scared off every bird in the neighborhood. The scream of the saw wound down to a series of sputters, then silence.

Mom set the chain saw gently down on the ground and casually brushed off her hands at a job well done. “There,” she said.

A few of the neighbors began to come forward.

I grabbed Mom by the arm and gave her a firm pull to get her started back to the house. As soon as she was walking along on her own, I stopped and turned around to address the murmurs that had already started. The last thing I needed was an angry mob following us home with questions about Mom's sanity, not to mention questions about what to do with the tree. I decided I had an answer for that, at least.

"You all need firewood, right?" I said. "The saw's right there. Help yourselves to it."

And with that, I continued on home, locking the front door behind me.

Pete got back from wherever he'd gone about an hour later. He was carrying not only his radio, but also a plastic bag.

"Where the heck were you?" I yelled at him.

Mom had gone back to bed without mentioning what she'd done, after I made her wash down a pill with a glass of water. I wondered how long it would take for her symptoms to wear off. Probably she'd have to be back on her pills for a while.

"At the library," Pete told me, his eyes narrowing in

confusion at my anger. "I got you a book. What happened outside? Who cut down that big tree?"

I looked in the bag and saw there a book by my favorite author, Jim Kjelgaard.

"It's *Outlaw Red*," said Pete. "I wasn't sure if you'd read that one."

I hadn't, but at that particular moment I didn't care. Beneath the book I saw the real reason that Pete had gone out, and why he hadn't been there for us when we needed him. He'd gone to find batteries. Breaking into the library had probably just been an afterthought.

I took the book out and threw it across the room, watched it collide with a picture of a sparrow that I had drawn for Mom a few months before, which she'd framed and put up on the wall above the lamp.

The picture fell, the glass breaking.

Story of my life. Story of all our lives.

THIRTY-EIGHT

They say that in certain species of hawks, the grasping instinct is so strong that sometimes they can't let go of their prey even if they need to, even if it becomes a matter of life and death. There are stories about northern goshawks being dragged underground while clutching large rabbits that kept on running after being caught, rabbits whose own instincts told them to seek safety inside their warrens.

The goshawk's wings would forcibly collapse as it entered the hole, the delicate bones all breaking on the way down, snapping like cheaply made kite frames, and still the hawk would not let go, its talons seeming to possess a will of their own. Once trapped, there was nothing the bird could do. It would either die there of its injuries or slowly starve to death. If it got lucky, a predator might come along and pull it free to kill it quickly and put it out of its misery.

The idea that a hawk might come to its end in such a tragic way disturbed me greatly, and confused me, too. How could an animal be so stupid? How could evolution allow for such behavior? I didn't understand that there was a very good reason this instinct was so strong, and that a firm grip could mean the difference between losing or keeping a meal, which in turn could mean the difference between survival and death. That's the thing about nature—it exists on a knife edge.

Humans used to exist on that edge, too, a long time ago. Maybe now we were beginning to feel the way that we used to, that it all could end at any moment unless we did something. Unless we grabbed on to a running rabbit and refused to let go.

I think the plan put forward by the voice on the radio became that rabbit.

There were debates, some of them escalating to

the point of violence. World leaders consulted with "experts," and those experts consulted with each other, and when the dust of all this lofty speculation finally settled, a reluctant consensus was met.

A date was set for the shattering. On September the third, at precisely four p.m., legions of people the world over would pick up their hammers and their bats, their golf clubs and tire irons, and together they would do the unthinkable.

I shivered at the thought of it.

September the third was only twelve days away. Just two hundred and eighty-eight short hours. I couldn't let it happen. I *wouldn't*.

Mom had been back on her pills for five days now and was already showing signs of improvement. Her headaches seemed less severe, and her tremors were almost gone. Still, I wasn't sure how long it would be before her mind was clear again. Probably more than twelve days, which meant that I might not be able to count on her to stand beside me on the day of the shattering. I might have to stop Pete all on my own, that or convince him to see things my way before that happened.

"It's not like we have to go along with it," I had

already tried to tell him. "It's not like it's a *law* or anything. Besides, Dad's only one person. One won't make any difference."

"What if everyone thought like that?" Pete asked me. "Then the shattering wouldn't work. One is *everything*, Ben. It's everything."

I could see then that my brother wasn't going to be swayed.

"Don't you at least feel bad about it?" I asked him.

He looked hurt, then angry. "It's not like I *want* to do this, Ben, but in case you hadn't noticed, it's the only plan we have. What do you think is going to happen if we just keep waiting? If we don't do anything at all? First we'll lose our electricity permanently. Then we'll lose our water. And what about food? Where would we get it from? How would we survive without any adults left in the world?"

"That wouldn't happen," I argued.

"Why? Because you don't want it to? That's not how life works, Ben. We don't get to just wish things into existence. Sometimes we have to make hard choices, for the good of everyone. If Dad was here, he'd say the same thing."

"He *is* here," I reminded him. "And don't tell me what he would say. You don't know that. Just because *you* think that the shattering is a good idea doesn't mean he would, too."

Pete shook his head, as if he felt sorry for me because I just wasn't getting it.

"It doesn't matter if it's a good idea, Ben. It's the only idea, and until someone else comes up with a *better* one, it's what we're stuck with."

"But it's *wrong*," I insisted. I couldn't get past this.

"That doesn't matter either," Pete said simply. "It's shades of gray, Ben. Shades of gray."

THIRTY-NINE

With only six days to go, the sky went dark and stayed that way. If you stood outside and listened closely, you could hear things, strange groaning noises, and creaks, like the hull of a submarine straining against the crushing weight of an ocean.

I looked at the sky and searched for cracks there, evidence that the other side might be breaking through now, one reality succumbing to another. I imagined galaxies colliding, moons and planets crumbling in the chaos, bright stars spiraling down into the awful depths of hungry black holes, their light being siphoned away like gas from a tank.

Never before had I felt so small and helpless, so alone.

My injuries were healing, but Mom looked them over anyway, her eyes so full of guilt that I almost cried for her.

"It's okay," I said.

"It's not okay," she whispered.

We didn't talk about the shattering. Not yet.

Dad was still in one piece, I kept reminding myself, and the cracks that I searched for in the sky above had not appeared. Hell on earth might be coming, but for now at least there was hope.

I began thinking that there had to be another way, if not of stopping the glass plague in its entirety, then at least of bringing Dad back before it was too late. I made it my mission to figure out how.

For lack of any other alternative, I went to the library. Mom wasn't happy about it, but she let me go anyway. I think she was beginning to understand that I wasn't the same eleven-year-old kid that I had been before. My childhood had effectively ended the moment that Dad turned to glass.

The lock on the library door was broken, so I walked right in. I wasn't sure if Pete had been the one to break it, or if someone had come before him, but I guess it didn't matter, just so long as the books were still there, which they were. So, too, was Ms. Golding, the librarian, her perfect posture preserved in glass behind her big desk.

I wandered the aisles with no clue where to begin, although not before depositing *Outlaw Red* in the return bin. I hadn't actually read it, but someday I might. Until then it would remain as something for me to look forward to, like how I looked forward to waxwings at the start of each winter. I think it's important to have things to look forward to, especially if you know that it's going to get cold and dark.

I turned my head sideways and read the book spines in search of inspiration. Nothing was jumping out at me, though. Still, I kept at it, knowing that persistence was something that Dad had always preached.

I lingered in the sections with paranormal and mythology books for a while, thinking about demons and angels and ghosts, and things like spells and wards and séances. Was there something I could use to protect Dad, or some way for me to communicate with him without *actually* communicating with him, like how a medium might talk to a spirit? I began pulling random books and skimming through pages, searching for step-by-step instructions and not just encyclopedic bits of information, which seemed to be what most of the books were full of.

What I needed was something specific, like an amateur's guide to communing, or a build-your-own-magical-amulets textbook, neither of which was likely to exist in the Griever's Mill Public Library. Heck, I already had to rely on interlibrary loans just to get my hands on some of the better bird books.

I began to pace, frustration building as I discarded one volume after another. A little voice in my head began telling me to just give up, to accept that anything a kid in a small-town library might possibly come up with had already been thought of and tried by folks much older and smarter than me.

I finally paused at the end of the aisle and looked again at Ms. Golding behind her desk. As always, she had a big scarf wrapped around her neck. She made them herself, and she seemed to have a new one every time I came to the library. The one she had on today was even larger than usual. It was red with yellow edges, and sort of reminded me of Doctor Strange's cape.

I bet he would know how to get Dad's soul back. I imagined the caped hero striking a magician's pose, his hands out before him, summoning cosmic energy to do with whatever he willed. If only it were that easy.

Poor Ms. Golding. She didn't have any kids, but I wondered if she had any pets. If so, they were probably starving now. Or maybe they were already dead.

Pete and I had a dog once, a black terrier named Buster. He was always getting out of the house and running off, until one day he got hit by a car. Pastor Nolan was nice enough to come over and hold a little doggie funeral for us. Afterward Pete asked him about ghosts. He wanted to know if dogs could become ghosts, too, or if it was only a human thing.

Pastor Nolan told him he wasn't sure, but that he believed that every living thing had a spirit.

"So, if dogs have spirits," Pete continued, "can they get possessed? Like that girl in *The Exorcist*?"

Dad had ended the conversation right there, apologizing for Pete's inappropriateness.

Pete had watched *The Exorcist* the week before while at a sleepover at his friend Shane's house. Shane's older brother had brought the movie home with him. He thought it might be worth a laugh to see how a pair of nine-year-olds reacted to it. He probably wasn't laughing when Shane's screams alerted their parents, though. Mom and Dad found out soon after, and Dad was livid. He grounded Pete for a month.

This all came back to me in an instant, the memory causing a light bulb to go off in my head. If regressions sometimes worked for those who'd returned, then maybe an exorcism might work for the ones who hadn't.

I wondered if Pastor Nolan had ever done one, and whether he even knew how. I almost went straight to his house to find out, but I'd already been gone for more than an hour and I knew that Mom might already be worrying. Besides, I wasn't sure if Pastor Nolan would even be at home. He might be at the church with Patrick.

I decided I would go first thing in the morning. I could get up early and leave Mom a note.

After feeling helpless for so long, it felt good to have an actual plan.

Pete was on his way up from the basement when I came in through the front door. He paused to look at me, but didn't ask where I'd been. Nor did I ask why he was carrying Dad's toolbox. We simply stared at each other for a moment, and then went about our separate business, which for Pete meant returning to our room (or, more accurately, to his radio), and for me meant heading into the dining room, to be close to Dad, and Mom as well, as it happened. For only the second time since Dad turned to glass, she was sitting with him at the dining room table.

She smiled at me as I approached. It was a tired smile, but tired in a normal way. She looked better.

"Did you find what you were looking for?" she asked.

I shook my head, deciding that I wasn't going to tell her about my exorcism idea just yet. I wanted to talk to Pastor Nolan first, to find out whether or not it was even possible. For all I knew, he'd already tried to do one on Patrick.

"It's okay," she told me. "You tried. Your dad would be proud of you for that."

"Would he?" I asked. I couldn't help but feel like I was letting him down, like there was a big doomsday clock hanging right over his head and the hands on it wouldn't stop moving.

"Of course," she assured me. She had her hands wrapped around a steaming mug.

"Tea?" I wondered if she'd found some in a place where I hadn't thought to look.

She shook her head. "Hot water with lemon. I couldn't find any tea. I guess we'll have to stop by Holga's one of these days."

I nodded and smiled, but didn't mention that her tea shop friend had packed up and left without saying good-bye.

"I'm gonna go downstairs and draw for a while," I said instead. I couldn't put my finger on exactly why, but something about Mom sitting there across from Dad was bothering me. It just seemed too normal. *Mom* seemed too normal. Like her mind had finally started to clear and she had decided that it was well past time to not only face what *was* happening, but what *might* happen from this point forward. If she got that far, I knew, then she would have to make a decision about the shattering.

"Okay, honey," she told me. "I'll call you when it's time for supper."

FORTY

I wasn't sure what to write on my note, so I decided to go with the truth. At least this way she wouldn't wonder and worry. I wrote:

Gone to see Pastor Nolan.
Be back soon.
-Ben

I left it on the counter where I knew Mom would find it, then slipped out the front door. I ran to the end of the block and stopped there for a second to look back and make sure Pete wasn't following me. He wasn't, so I continued on.

Pastor Nolan lived about halfway along Chester Street, in a small blue-and-white bungalow with a red-brick chimney. I'd never been inside his house, but it was easy to remember which one it was because the place right next to it was a weird pinkish-purple color, and belonged to a woman named Mrs. De Lint, who everyone knew because she owned a skunk named Pepper as a pet. She walked it around town on a leash, like a dog. People sometimes ran away from it, even though it had been de-stinked.

I walked up Pastor Nolan's sidewalk and thought about what I would say. I wasn't sure I should use the word *exorcism* right off the bat. Working up to it would probably be better.

I rang the bell and waited.

I hadn't actually seen Pastor Nolan since that day at church when Patrick was taken, so I didn't really know what to expect if he answered the door. I imagined an unshaven wreck who hadn't slept for more than a week, eyes all glossy and red, crisp white collar dulled to gray. Or maybe he wouldn't be home at all. Maybe he was staying at the church to be close to his son, still frozen in place atop his organ bench, a lumberjack statue with musical hands.

I rang the doorbell a second time, and knocked, too, in case the buzzer wasn't working.

"Pastor Nolan?" I finally yelled, my face right up to the door. "Are you in there? It's me, Ben Cameron, from church. I need to talk to you."

Even if he couldn't help me with an exorcism, maybe he could at least come over and have a talk with Mom and Pete. Maybe he could try to convince my brother to have some faith in something other than the Voice.

I waited. Still nothing.

I sighed, thinking that I'd have to go all the way to the church now. Before I did, though, I decided to check the door. I was pretty sure it would be locked, but it wasn't. It swung inward with the faintest creak.

"Pastor Nolan?" I said again. It felt wrong to go beyond the threshold, so I held back for a moment, until a bad feeling came over me, compelling me farther. I stepped lightly through the gray-carpeted living room and turned right into a bright and spacious kitchen. The house was silent, the rooms dark but tidy. Nothing appeared unkempt or out of place. There wasn't even a single dirty dish in the sink, but for some reason my bad feeling intensified.

I continued into the hallway, passing first a bathroom and then a reading room before finally arriving at what I assumed must be Pastor Nolan's bedroom. The door was halfway closed, blocking my view. My heart pounded as I reached up to push it open.

Pastor Nolan stood frozen next to his bed. He was facing a full-length mirror, his left arm down at his side, clutching a rosary, and his right arm reaching, as if the act of touching his own reflection might somehow keep him from turning to glass, which it obviously hadn't. He was wearing his cassock, his skin now as dark as the flowing black fabric itself. The white swatch on his collar seemed strangely isolated.

I looked down at the dangling cross on the rosary, and felt all my hope flow right out of me, like air from a punctured bike tube. Finding the tea shop empty had been a disappointment; this was like a death blow. My plan was ruined now, and there was no time to come up with a new one. Not that an exorcism was likely to have worked anyway. Maybe I'd just been lying to myself so I wouldn't have to face the truth.

I stood there for a moment, not knowing what to do next. There was an open window on the opposite side of the bed, with thin white curtains that were sweeping in and out across the sill at the whim of the wind. I watched the back-and-forth motion for maybe a minute, until a strong gust of wind finally broke the spell and sent the curtain fluttering inward like some Halloween ghost. The spectral illusion lasted only a moment, the curtain settling back into its rhythm as the wind eased up some.

I'm not sure why, but I went over to close the sash. A sound from outside, however, stopped me. It was the sound of birds, the familiar *chip*s and *jib*s of sparrows conversing. House sparrows.

I looked outside and saw three large feeders there, swinging in the wind beneath an apple tree laden with overripe fruit. Several birds were perched amidst the branches. I felt a surge of hope at the sight of them, my first thought being that maybe these were Mom's sparrows, come to visit the pastor's yard, only there wasn't a leucistic female among them. I searched for the pure white wings to no avail.

The birds darted away as soon as they noticed me, seeking shelter in a globe cedar that was likely their home.

No, I thought, *these aren't Mom's sparrows*. These ones belonged here, and had probably been here their whole lives, or at least for as long as the feeders had been up.

Soon they would need to find a new home, now that Pastor Nolan would no longer be around to replenish the seeds. I imagined house sparrows all over the world becoming displaced in this way, moving from one backyard to the next like winged refugees, their human providers vanishing one by one, from flesh to glass, soul by mortal soul.

What would happen to house sparrows as a species if people disappeared entirely? Would they follow us into oblivion, slowly but surely, as wilder species moved in to reclaim our towns and cities? That's the thing about house sparrows—they've kind of evolved alongside us, building their homes by our homes, sharing our space and our food, hanging out in our parking lots like a bunch of kids with no place else to go.

If you drive out into the country, you'll hardly see them at all. The nest boxes you find along the back roads will be filled with swallows and bluebirds, and sparrows of the American variety, like Savannah and vesper and lark sparrows. *True* sparrows, some might say, as the "house" variety aren't technically sparrows at all. They actually belong to the weaver-finch family. The settlers renamed them after bringing them here from overseas, because their coloration was so similar to that of the native sparrows. The birds were supposed to help in controlling insect pest populations, only it didn't quite work out that way. As it turned out, house sparrows usually prefer seeds and grains to bugs. Still, the birds thrived and were soon riding railcars from one settlement to the next, traveling along with their favorite food sources and establishing their own little colonies inside ours. They've been our constant companions ever since, succeeding wherever we do, and sometimes failing right alongside us.

I wondered if, on some level, the birds understood this, that our fates had become intertwined. If so, how would they adapt? What would they do? Was there anything they even *could* do? It wasn't as if a few lowly house sparrows had the power to stop the glass plague, although maybe they could mob the crows who came to carry our souls away after we transformed, the same way they banded together to mob crows who tried to rob nests. Maybe they could start getting crows to leave souls behind, or maybe the sparrows could even follow crows from this world into the next one and, once there, steal souls and bring them back.

That last thought hit me like an epiphany as I remembered that Mom's sparrows had disappeared at pretty much exactly the same time that Dad turned to glass. It was almost as if they'd gone with him, or *after* him, perhaps. Maybe Mom's sparrows were the first to sense what was coming, and therefore the first to act. Maybe if we just waited a little while longer, they would return and Dad would be whole again.

I looked back at Pastor Nolan, reaching toward the mirror and his reflection reaching back, like Adam and

God in that famous old painting. The hopelessness that I'd felt when I entered the room was gone now, replaced by a faith in something that might be unlikely, but at least seemed possible. All I had to do was tell Mom, and together we could overrule Pete.

I left Pastor Nolan's and ran for home.

FORTY-ONE

I entered the house and kicked off my shoes, fully expecting that Mom would be waiting for me and wondering why I would have gone to see our pastor so early in the morning, but she wasn't. The living room and kitchen were empty, and, as usual, Dad was alone and unchanged at the table in the dining room. I checked the backyard bench, but she wasn't there either.

I went over to the bottom of the stairs and was just about to call up to her when I heard something that stopped me cold: an unfamiliar voice from up in Pete's and my room. A man's voice.

I held my breath, my pulse quickening. I listened for a second but couldn't make out his words. Whoever it was, neither Pete nor Mom was talking back, which I took to be a bad sign, as if they'd been *told* to be quiet. I immediately pictured some crazed lunatic, holding a finger to his lips and a knife in his hand, one of those Rambo-style ones with a blade on one side and a row of sawing teeth on the other.

In spite of this all-too-vivid image, I continued up to the top of the stairs, taking care not to step on the creaky spots. The voice continued to talk, but there was a muffled quality to the sound, as well as a soft and steady background hiss, the hiss—it suddenly dawned on me—of radio static.

I opened the door, my heart sinking at what I found on the other side.

Pete's radio was sitting in the middle of the floor. Its plastic shell had been removed and wires spilled out from inside it—wires that Pete had cut and then spliced together with others, bypassing the radio's blown speaker for one that worked properly—a rectangular tower that stood next to Dad's toolbox.

Pete was in his usual spot on the floor, his back up

against the side of his mattress and box spring. Mom was sitting on the edge of my bed with her hands folded neatly in her lap. It didn't look like she'd just sat down. Her posture was too settled, her attention too focused. She had obviously been listening for a while.

"What's going on?" I asked. I could only imagine what the voice on the radio had filled her head with. I felt my jaw clench at the thought of it.

"Sit down, Ben," Mom told me. "I think it's time we had a family talk."

It wasn't so much her words that shook me (although they did), but more her expression. I'd seen the same one on Pete's face for days, a mixture of pity and hard resolve.

I shook my head and went no farther, my horror at this new development mixing with a wary surprise at the reasoned tone of the voice on the radio. I guess I'd just imagined something more impassioned, something with more fire and wild intensity, sort of like you might get from a fanatical preacher in a movie. This wasn't that at all, though. This was more the voice of a teacher or a philosopher, of a scientist and a sage all wrapped into one. Somehow that made it even scarier.

"No!" I tried to tell Mom. "You don't understand! The sparrows went after him! We have to wait!" My knees suddenly grew so weak that I had to lean against the door to keep myself from falling.

Mom stood up and reached out for me, sympathy in her eyes. "Oh, Ben" was all she said to me. "Oh, Ben."

FORTY-TWO

I tried to explain it all downstairs, where I wouldn't have to compete with another voice. Mom listened as I pieced it all together, and although there was a moment when an ember of hope seemed to spark in her eyes, an instant in which she believed me, or at least *wanted* to believe me, the fire of certainty never quite kindled.

"It's a nice thought, Ben," she finally told me. "But I'm not sure it's anything more than that."

Pete wasn't nearly so kind.

"Sparrows?" he scoffed. "We're supposed to wait

because of some stupid sparrows? You gotta be kidding me."

I felt like Mom had pushed me down and Pete had kicked me in the stomach, all while Dad sat helplessly by, still saying grace after all this time.

Of course I was serious. I'd never been more serious about anything in my life, and I didn't understand how Pete could be so dismissive. After all, he himself had seen the way that the crows always seemed to show up right after a transformation, first the one that landed on old man Crandall's head, and then the small murder of them right outside the church that day. We hadn't actually seen one when Dad turned, but the single caw that had come from outside was unmistakable. It couldn't just be a coincidence. It meant something. It had to. And if crows and ravens could move between worlds, then why couldn't sparrows? Maybe all birds could. It was just that most of them didn't have any reason to.

I stared at my older brother, my frustration turning to anger now, and suspicion. I couldn't ignore the fact that Pete and Dad had never gotten along, that there had always been a weird sort of tension whenever the two of them were in the same room.

"Do you even care that he's gone?" I asked him. "Do you even miss him?" I wanted to hurt him. I wanted him to feel as awful in that moment as I did.

"Ben!" said Mom, shocked at my words. Pete just stood there, though, his expression softening.

"Of course I miss him," he told me. "Of course I care. But I also care about you and Mom. That's why we need to do something. Wishes aren't plans, Ben. Maybe you're still too young to understand that."

"I understand it just fine," I told him. "You're the one who needs to grow up a little."

Pete just shook his head, as if to say that he wasn't taking the bait.

I turned to Mom then, imploring her with only my eyes since I wasn't sure I could talk and not start crying.

"There's still time, Ben," she told me. "We have five more days yet. If you're right, then maybe that's all the time we'll need. We just have to wait and see."

If she was hoping to reassure me, she didn't succeed. I understood now that, like Pete, she had made up her mind. For a brief moment, I wished she'd never started back on her pills. At least then Pete would still be alone in his convictions. But then I remembered how weak and shaky she had been, and how she had looked on the morning that she picked up the chain saw, with empty madness in her eyes and cold instant coffee dribbling down her chin. It was an image I didn't think I'd ever be able to get out of my mind, and one that I hoped I would never have to see again.

I couldn't look at either of them anymore and felt claustrophobic just sharing a room with them. I started toward the back door, Mom telling me to please wait, to please not go. I paused to look at her, making no effort to hide the anger on my face. I looked at Pete, too, who was sitting across the room from me, near the fireplace. It suddenly occurred to me that I was a lot closer to his radio than he was. Although breaking it probably wouldn't serve any real purpose now that a date and a time for the shattering had already been set, it would probably feel pretty darn good to see it in pieces.

My gaze remained on Pete but my body started to turn, toward the stairwell.

He narrowed his eyes at me. "Don't do it, Ben," he warned me.

I hesitated for only a second, then shot for the stairs, taking them two at a time while Pete charged after me.

I managed to get to the radio an instant before he got to me, but all I had time to do was pick it up and hurl it toward the wall, the spliced wires coming apart as I did so, the new tower speaker toppling over as the body of the radio itself—still missing its outer shell—collided with one of Pete's muscle car posters and then fell to the floor, leaving behind it a loose flap of ripped paper where before there had been a shiny chrome wheel. The voice went silent.

Pete shoved me out of his way, swearing a blue streak.

I laughed for a second, and then started to cry, the pointlessness of it all washing over me.

FORTY-THREE

Pete locked himself in our bedroom with the toolbox and radio. I wasn't really sure how badly I'd damaged it, but I figured it was mostly cosmetic. The voice would probably be speaking again in no time. Meanwhile, all I could do was just fume and pace, and berate myself for not trying to destroy the thing sooner, when I first got the inkling that something was wrong.

Mom tried to get me to eat something. My stomach was growling so loud that she actually heard it, and yet the thought of eating just made me feel gross. Food could wait. What I really needed was some air, so I went outside and sat on the step, the ashen sky softly groaning and creaking above me. My face felt hot, flushed. My leg bounced with nervous energy. I put my head in my hands and stared out at nothing.

A moment later a black-and-white shape entered my peripheral vision. I sat up and looked, saw movement beside an overturned garbage can. It was a skunk, I realized, but not just some random wild one out scavenging for scraps. It was Pepper, the skunk that lived in the pinkish-purple house right beside Pastor Nolan's. It was wearing a collar—purple like the house it belonged in, with small diamond studs that would have caught the light had the sun not been permanently quarantined. The skunk paused when it noticed me watching it, but it didn't run. Pepper was friendly and trusting of humans. Mrs. De Lint had let me pet it one time, and I could still remember how that big fluffy tail felt under my fingers. Was it possible that Pepper remembered me, too?

I got up and approached, and tried talking to it in a low soft voice, saying, "Hey, Pepper. What are you doing out here all alone?"

The skunk just looked at me, its dark eyes glistening. Clearly it had gotten out somehow (like our old dog, Buster, always used to) and wandered away from its neighborhood. I wondered if skunks could find their way home the same way cats did. If not, then Pepper would need my help.

"Should we find you a leash?" I said, looking around the yard for something to use. My eyes came to rest on a long piece of twine that one of our bird feeders was hanging from. I went over and quickly untied it, while Pepper continued to investigate the contents of the overturned can.

I got the twine free and left the bird feeder crammed in a nook between two branches. As I turned back around, the dark sky swirled and shifted so abruptly that I felt for a second like I was standing on a moving platform. I had to pause to let a moment of vertigo pass.

I wasn't sure how the skunk would react to me coming close enough to actually reach down and grab its collar, but as it turned out, it hardly reacted at all. In fact, it seemed happy for the human touch. I tied one end of the twine to the collar and wrapped the other end twice around my palm, and that was that; we were ready to go.

"Come straight home again," said Mom from the

doorway. I hadn't realized she'd been watching me. I held her gaze for a moment but didn't reply, and then Pepper and I were off, a sad and hopeless-feeling eleven-year-old and a lost skunk on a leash made of twine, both of us beneath a strange sky in a town full of people who had turned to glass.

Walking a skunk, I discovered, was a lot like walking a dog. Pepper's nose did the leading, and it stopped to investigate almost every new thing it encountered. I took advantage of each brief pause to scan the trees for late-summer warblers, which should have started moving south already. But there was no sign of them. For the first time I wondered if the constant darkness might have an effect on bird migration. I hoped not.

Slowly but surely, we plodded along, ten minutes bringing us halfway to where we were going. We turned onto a street that looked even more abandoned than the last few that we had gone down. Out of twelve houses, I counted only two with cars in driveways. There was one bike as well, a BMX left carelessly on the edge of a lawn up ahead. I didn't think anything of it until I reached it and recognized the bike as belonging to Lars Messam.

I quickly glanced up and over at the front door to the house. It was one of those doors that had a bunch of little windows in it, each rectangle of glass framed by decorative metal trim. One of these little windows—the one closest to the handle and the dead bolt—was smashed. I shook my head. Lars was looting, and during the daytime no less. This was bold, even for one of the Messam twins.

I watched the house for a moment before deciding that I'd best keep moving, not only for my sake, but also Pepper's. I hadn't forgotten what I'd found in the sandbox-turned-firepit in the Messams' backyard. I took a step forward and gave the leash a gentle tug, and that's when the front door of the house swung open and Lars leaned out to drop a stuffed backpack onto the step. He didn't look up or see me, but instead disappeared back inside.

My heart kicked against my rib cage at the close call, this while my brain played a loop of a wagging finger and the promise of *Next time. Next time.*

I tugged the twine leash again, but this time Pepper resisted. The skunk had apparently decided that this was the perfect place to stop and take care of business.

“Really?” I said. “Right now?”

I glanced back at the house, feeling suddenly exposed and vulnerable. There was movement in the window. I crouched low to make myself smaller, but Lars wasn’t looking out at me. He was doing something with the curtains. I narrowed my eyes, wondering what. A second later I had my answer, as an expanding circle of flame began to consume the draping fabric. Lars had apparently made up his mind that simply looting the place wasn’t enough.

All the stories that had been in the news about whole city blocks going up in smoke suddenly came back to me. I could already see it happening, the way the fire would leap unimpeded from one house right to the next, down the whole length of the street. It obviously hadn’t occurred to Lars, but if this one fire was left to burn, our entire town might end up as a pile of smoldering embers.

I rushed Pepper over to the yard next door and quickly looped the twine around the top of a fire hydrant, then I turned and made a beeline across the yard and into the house, just as Lars was leaving, a big proud grin on his face. The grin disappeared when he saw me, his impish delight replaced with a look of surprise and confusion. I shot him a glare in passing but kept on going. There was no time to stop.

The fire was still growing and climbing toward the ceiling, but the bottom corners of both of the curtains remained unburned. I reached down, grabbed them, and pulled, the wavering wall of fire falling toward me as the rings at the top broke free from the rod. The sudden release threw me totally off balance. I stumbled backward, but somehow still managed to duck out of the way just in time to avoid having my hair go up like a torch.

Lars had come back in and was yelling at me, demanding to know what I was doing, while shuffle-stepping to keep a safe distance from his own idiotic handiwork, which threatened to spread to the rug and the couch.

"What does it look like I'm doing?!" I yelled back. I tried stomping the fire to put it out, but my shoes weren't doing the job, so I grabbed a cushion from the couch and started smothering the flames with that. It was a lot bigger than my size 6s.

Between the arching flames and those I managed to put out, the smoke thickened around me, to the point where I could hardly breathe.

Lars started to laugh. I was pretty sure I heard him slap his knee.

"Help me, you moron!" I coughed at him. "The whole neighborhood's gonna burn down! Don't you know that there aren't any firefighters anymore?" I wasn't sure this was strictly true, but given that Griever's Mill's firefighters were all volunteers—Dad being one of them—I was pretty sure no one was coming.

Lars stopped laughing then and seemed to consider this. Was it really possible that he'd thought the fire would remain in one place, consuming a single house as if it were isolated in a brick-lined pit? The other alternative was that he hadn't thought about it at all, that he'd lit the fire on a whim, with zero consideration as to what might happen next.

Judging by the look on his face now, I figured it must be the second thing. But he didn't step forward to help me. He just stood there and stupidly stared down at his fire, which had just found its way onto my pant leg. I didn't notice until I felt the heat, and I swore as I snuffed it out, the fabric molten against my leg. In an anger- and panic-fueled flurry, I grabbed more cushions and kept up my smothering attack, robbing the flames of oxygen while struggling to get enough of my own. It took some doing, but I finally managed to get it all out.

I doubled over, coughing harder than I had ever coughed in my life.

When at last I straightened back up again, Lars was still just standing there, a twelve-year-old punk with a soul as black as tar. He looked at me and said, "I suppose you think you're a hero now or something."

It was exactly the sort of thing that I would have expected him to say, only instead of it coming across as intimidating or antagonistic, it now just seemed pathetic and sad, and the more I thought about it, the more I realized that those were the only two words I needed to describe the twins. Maybe it was because I was having a particularly awful day, or maybe it was the end result of everything that I had been through since the glass plague started, both at home and everywhere else, but suddenly words like *tough* and *scary* didn't seem to apply. The image I'd built up in my mind was starting to crumble.

We stared at each other across a distance of less than ten feet, and it was in that exact moment, as our eyes locked in the thinning smoke, that I lost all fear of

Lars Messam. I felt it leave me like a weight, freeing me. I had already stood up to him once inside the tea shop when last we crossed paths, but that was different; that was anger and spite toward Pete just redirected, and desperation masked as courage. This was something more permanent. The predator/prey dynamic was broken, and I could tell that Lars sensed it, too. I saw it in his posture and his eyes, and though I thought he might still block me as I made for the door, he didn't. I walked right past him as if he weren't even there, and then I was down the steps and crossing the yard to where a lost skunk waited for an escort home.

The sky churned and a crow flew past me, cawing as I took up the twine. I didn't bother turning around to see where it landed or why it was there. I already knew.

FORTY-FOUR

Pete had the radio fixed by the time I got home. I could hear it even before I got through the door, but I went in anyway, wondering again how just one voice could do so much talking, and how just one man could convince so many that he was right when I couldn't even convince two just to keep their minds open to other ideas, like how a small flock of sparrows might help themselves by trying to help us.

I reeked of smoke and my jeans were ruined, and my leg didn't feel great either. Mrs. De Lint had asked me if I'd rescued Pepper from a burning building. When I told her no, she was understandably confused. So was Mom. She immediately wanted to know where I'd been and what I'd been doing. I told her it was nothing and that I was fine, even as I marched upstairs and into the bathroom to put on some salve and a wrap. Mom wasn't about to let me off that easy, though. She followed me up and stood just outside the door.

"If you started a fire, Ben," she said, "I need to know about it."

I felt angry and hurt at the assumption.

"I was putting it *out*," I said shortly. "Just like *Dad* would have."

There was a moment of silence. "Okay, good," she said. "That's good. You can still talk to me, you know. It doesn't have to be like this."

I didn't answer her. The voice droned on from across the hall, saying something about strength of purpose. I clucked my tongue inside my mouth in an effort to drown out the words.

Mom waited for an answer that wasn't coming. Then I heard her sigh. "When you're done in there, come downstairs please," she told me. "I don't care if you want to or not, you need to eat something."

She was right. My empty stomach had gone from growling to feeling like it was starting to digest itself. First things first, though. I rolled up my pant leg and put on some salve. It felt cool against my skin, which was red but hadn't blistered. I guessed that meant the burn wasn't really that bad. The wrap went on next. I did it too tight the first time and had to start over, but other than that, it all went fine.

I thought about changing into some clean clothes, but since that would have required me going into my room, I settled for some less dirty ones out of the hamper in the basement. Afterward, I ate some beans and a handful of dried banana chips. As I chewed I realized that I hadn't brushed my teeth in days. My hair was in dire need of washing, too. I suddenly felt as uncomfortable in my skin as I did in my house. And Pete was only making things worse.

The voice got louder as he opened the bedroom door upstairs. I waited for him to close it again, but he didn't. I wasn't sure if this was a dare or an invitation, but either way, I wasn't biting. Instead I waited until Mom had her back turned (there was no way she was going to let me leave again after seeing the state I'd just come home in) and then grabbed both sets of Dad's truck keys from the hook in the hallway and quickly snuck outside.

I didn't actually need the keys, since Dad always left the truck open, but I figured this way I could lock myself in and stay there as long as I wanted.

As always, the truck smelled of Armor All and Old Spice and air-freshener pine. This was the first time I'd been in it since Dad was transformed, and I wasn't prepared for the flood of memories that the familiar scents triggered. From camping and fishing trips to drives to the rink and runs into Paulson for the annual midway and once every winter to pick out a tree. I'd never really thought about it before, but the truck was sort of our ticket to escaping the monotony of our small-town world. I wondered if we would ever escape it again.

I took hold of the wheel and squeezed it as hard as I could, willing my hurt and frustration to bleed from my fingers and into the old worn leather.

Mom came out and knocked on the passenger window. "Can we please not do this, Ben?" she said. "It's getting late. I know things are hard for you right now, but I'd like you to come back inside."

The darkness of day was giving way to the darkness of night now, gray becoming black as the sky continued with its low groans and unnerving creaks. I thought back to the afternoon when all this started, when we got home from the garage and Mom came running out of the house and looked up as if the sky were falling. It almost seemed like it might now, like huge chunks of it could start raining down at any moment. I almost wished that it would. I was tired of being crushed slowly.

"Not until you and Pete promise not to touch Dad," I replied.

"You know I can't promise that, Ben," she told me.

"Fine," I said. "I'm staying here, then." I felt like a child, demanding to have my way. I wasn't, though. Not anymore.

Mom crossed her arms. "I'll give you ten minutes," she told me. "Ten minutes more and that's it."

I watched her return to the house. The night continued to deepen around me. Twice, the streetlights flickered as power tried and failed to restore itself. I felt as if a similar flickering and failing had been happening inside me, as every idea I had to make things better seemed destined to just fizzle out. I know my dad would have told me not to give up, but without a little luck or some help, I wasn't sure that there was much left I could do.

As if in answer to this thought, I heard a car approaching from down the street. The truck was facing the house, so I had to turn around in my seat to see who it was. Constable Sheery's cruiser rolled past a moment later, the sight of it instantly bringing to mind what Dad had said to us that day when we eavesdropped on him from upstairs, and how if worse ever came to worst, we could always call on Wayne Sheery for help.

Hoping that Dad was right, I jumped out of the truck and ran into the street, waving my arms like someone in need of a rescue. I wasn't sure if he'd be able to see me in the growing dark, so I started yelling, too, saying, "Stop! Wait! Over here!" The brake lights came on as the car slowed down, and then sure enough it pulled a U-turn at the end of the street and started coming back toward me.

Yes! I thought, simultaneously relieved and excited at the fact that something was finally going my way. I wasn't sure yet exactly *how* Constable Sheery might be able to help me, but help me he would, of that much I was certain. He wasn't just a cop, after all. He was also Dad's friend.

I waved again once the car had covered about half the distance back to our house, but then something strange happened. Instead of slowing down, the car sprang forward, like Constable Sheery had stomped on the gas. It swerved a little, too, so that suddenly both of its headlights had me pinned.

I stopped waving but still had my hand up, confusion freezing me in place. I couldn't understand why he wasn't hitting the brakes or correcting his course. The closer he got, the more the car picked up speed, the engine roaring.

The gears in my brain still hadn't engaged yet, but thankfully my muscles recognized the danger. Without consciously thinking about it, I jumped back and out of the path of the runaway cruiser just in time. The streetlamps flickered the moment it passed me, the brief flashes of light shining on Constable Sheery's face. His skin was shiny and black, his expression a frozen rictus of panic and fear. He must have lost control when he felt himself changing, his arms seizing up while the foot that he drove with became a heavy dead weight on the pedal.

With a crunch and a squeal of metal on metal, the cruiser glanced off the side of Uncle Dean's pickup truck and kept on going right down the street, where it pinballed off two other parked cars before finally plowing headlong into the back of a big fifth-wheel trailer near the end of the block. The impact was like a cannon going off in the night, and somehow set off the cruiser's siren, albeit only for a few seconds. It wailed discordantly and then died.

I hadn't seen or heard her coming, but suddenly Mom was beside me, her eyes wide with shock and worry as she helped me up from the grass. She kept asking me if I was all right. I gave her a blank nod, my ears still ringing from the crash and the siren.

As soon as I was steady on my feet and it was clear that I really was okay, Mom told me to wait right there and said she needed to go and check if Constable Sheery was okay.

She was off and running before I could tell her that

there was no point, that even with an airbag to cushion him, Wayne Sheery was surely now just a fragmented pile on the seat and the floor.

I turned and headed back to the house, my gaze traveling up to our bedroom window, where Pete stood in still silhouette against the light of several candles.

FORTY-FIVE

I barely slept for the next three nights, and when I did, I dreamed of sparrows, lost and flying through a maelstrom, their wings and tail feathers battered by winds so strong that I could still hear the roar in my ears even after waking. I had my sleeping bag down on the floor right next to the dining room table now. I'd given up my chair by the window in order to be closer to Dad.

Pete wasn't sleeping much either. I could hear him pacing up in our room, back and forth and back and forth, as if the accumulation of steps might somehow absolve him of some of his guilt. I also noticed that he wasn't eating much, or listening to his radio quite as often as he had been, perhaps because he could no longer carry it on his shoulder, or perhaps because he was starting to have second thoughts. Maybe now that we were coming down to it, the true gravity of the situation was beginning to assert its pull.

I started catching him taking sidelong glances at Dad, his eyes filled with a wary uncertainty. He didn't just look tired; he looked absolutely wrecked, and maybe even a tad bit out of his mind, which made me wonder if the little sleep that he actually was getting was filled with nightmares. The kind you can't quite shake even after waking. Maybe his subconscious was trying to tell him something, planting seeds that I might just be able to water.

I needed to confront him again, but I had to be careful. I couldn't just ask him if he was having doubts, or tell him that there was still time to change his mind. I had to be cleverer than that. I had to offer him a way out that didn't require him to admit that he might have been wrong in the first place.

"I'll challenge you for it," I finally told him.

I found him outside on the lawn, craning his neck

toward a sky that looked like a liquid bruise and sounded like a steel bridge on the verge of collapse. It was impossible to get used to, that sound; my muscles instinctively tensed with every new creak. This was the loudest I'd ever heard it.

"Challenge me for what?" Pete asked. The bags under his eyes looked even darker outside than they had in the house. His hair was a total catastrophe.

"For Dad," I told him. "Propeller leaves. If yours lands closest to the X, we'll go through with the shattering. If mine does, we'll wait."

He stared at me. "You're serious," he said. It wasn't a question.

I nodded. It was the only idea I had.

"Let's let fate decide," I told him. "Whatever is meant to happen, will."

He continued staring at me. "That's crazy."

Invisible girders sagged above us. *Crik...crik... crik...crack...*

We both looked up. We couldn't help it. The liquid bruise continued to swirl. I imagined for a second that Pete and I were standing on Jupiter instead of Earth, gazing up at the gas giant's big dark eye, watching it watch us.

"Fine," Pete said, his eyes still trained on the sky. "When?"

I was so stunned that it took me a second to reply.

"Right now," I said, my heart already pounding in anticipation.

"Okay," said Pete. "Sure." He seemed a little stunned himself, as if his mouth had made a decision before his brain had had a chance to think it through. "Should we tell Mom?"

I shook my head. "I just need to get my shoes." Pete already had his on, but I had come out in my socks. My foot had only just healed from stepping on the rake, but apparently I hadn't learned my lesson yet.

I ran inside and laced up, but not before grabbing the maple seedpod that I had saved from the day that old man Crandall turned to glass, along with the white chalk that we'd used to draw our last sidewalk X.

Pete found his own maple seedpod along the way, neither one of us talking at all, just marching like a pair of soldiers toward our doom.

FORTY-SIX

"Are you sure you want to do this?" Pete asked me.

I stared down at the freshly drawn X inside a circle on the concrete below, only now fully appreciating what I was gambling on. What other choice did I have?

I took a deep breath and nodded, the wind whipping my hair about my face. It seemed to be blowing from every direction at once, making it impossible to try to predict which way a seedpod might fall.

Strangely, Pete didn't seem worried at all. If anything, he just looked resigned, as if it didn't matter who won, as if we'd both be losing either way, which maybe was true, although I was trying not to think like that. In spite of everything, I was trying to think positively.

"I'll go first," Pete offered.

I shook my head. "Uh-uh. We'll both go at the same time."

Pete narrowed his eyes. "That's not how we do it. You can't just change the rules."

"It's the fairest way," I said.

"How will we tell them apart?" he asked me.

"I'll mark mine with chalk," I said.

He looked at me uncertainly, and for the briefest of moments, a split second at most, I thought about pushing him, and imagined him going over the edge, his body landing flat on the X.

"Fine," he agreed. "Let's just get it over with."

My seedpod was dry and fragile, so I had to be careful pressing down with the chalk. It didn't help that I was nervous and shaking, too, but I finally managed to make a visible mark on the thickest part of it, where the seed itself was encased.

"On three?" I said, leaning forward.

"On three," Pete agreed.

We counted together: "One, two, three..."

Our propellers were off and spinning, the speed of rotation immediately rendering my white mark invisible. Still, it was easy to tell them apart to begin with, as both of them spun away from each other, mine going north as Pete's went south. Seconds later, however, they both changed course and crossed paths before getting caught in the very same eddy, which sent them around and around each other, too fast for my eyes to follow, and yet at the same time, eerily slow, like two ships caught in a whirlpool of molasses.

I thought of Dad the entire time, remembering how he'd once told us that the most generous thing you could give to a person was your time. It seemed cruelly ironic to me that time was now the thing that Dad needed most.

Down and down the seedpods went, and for a second it looked like *both* of them would land on the bull's-eye, either right beside each other or right on top of each other, but then they collided, one of them falling just left of the center of the X and the other just to the right of it.

Pete and I both leaned forward, squinting. I could just barely make out my white mark now, but it didn't matter; it was too close to call from up on the roof.

"Huh," said Pete. "That's never happened before."

The sky *crik-crik-crack*ed as if in reply.

We ran to the ladder and made our way down and around to the front of the shop. Pete stood on one side of the landing pad and I stood on the other, both of us bending over with our hands on our knees, the tops of our heads almost touching. I still couldn't tell which of the seedpods was closest. Pete couldn't either.

"Let's measure it in chalk lengths," he suggested.

"Good idea."

But before I could even get the chalk out of my pocket, the wind swirled again and picked up both of our seedpods, carrying them away along with a bunch of dry leaves and dust from the street. I squinted against the sudden onslaught of debris, my brain struggling to make any sense of what had just happened.

"Now what?" Pete asked.

"We'll find new ones and go again," I said.

Pete looked down at the empty landing pad a moment longer and then slowly shook his head. "Uh-uh," he said.

I narrowed my eyes. "Why not?"

"Fate was supposed to decide," he replied. "But obviously fate doesn't want to. We asked for an answer and never got one."

"Doesn't mean we can't ask again."

He looked at me, his eyes now filled with a peculiar sort of clarity, as if everything suddenly made perfect sense to him. "That's just it," he told me. "We should never have asked in the first place. This is way too big to just leave up to chance."

"So why'd you even come?" I asked him.

"I don't know," he admitted. "I guess I was confused. I guess I just needed to see what would happen."

I shook my head, the frustration I'd been feeling for days returning instantly. I was mad, too, not just at the fact that Pete wouldn't try again, but also at his sudden certainty, as if the universe had just whispered wisdom into his ear when in reality the wind had thrown crap at him.

"You're still going to try to stop me, aren't you?" he asked me.

I crossed my arms but didn't say anything, which I guess was answer enough.

Pete sighed. "All you're doing is making it harder on yourself. And harder on Mom, too."

"Someone needs to be on Dad's side," I said.

"Dad's gone, Ben, and he's not coming back. It's like when a cicada molts and leaves its old shell behind."

"If you really thought it was like that, then you wouldn't be here."

"I was confused," he said again. "I had a moment of weakness."

"But now you're better," I said sarcastically.

"I'm not gonna stand here arguing with you," he told me. "I'm done, and I'm going home. Are you coming?"

I shook my head. "Not with you," I told him. There was no way I could walk beside him now, as if it were old times, and all we'd been doing was just hanging out together, talking about comic books and *Star Wars* beneath an innocent summer sky. We were on Jupiter now, I reminded myself, and my brother was no longer my brother. He was my enemy.

FORTY-SEVEN

As strange as it would seem to me later when I looked back on it, the day before the shattering was eerily calm, peaceful even.

I held firm to my belief that the plan was wrong, and Pete remained convinced that it didn't matter, that we had to go through with it anyway. It was our only option. Our lines had been drawn in the sand, and so tomorrow I would take my stand against my brother. Today, however, I would simply be there for Dad—not angry or desperate or frustrated (although I was all those things underneath), but simply present, a body in a chair beside another body in a chair.

I thought again of our sparrows, and silently willed the universe to provide them with some direction, since the dreams that I'd been having seemed to be telling me they had gotten lost. I kept looking for them through the window, but so far all I'd seen were chickadees.

Mom went out and filled the feeders just before lunch, pausing for a while at each one, her eyes scanning the trees and the bushes, her expression never changing, except once when the merlin flew over, as silent and deadly as she had ever been. Mom looked up and a small smile appeared. I think she was glad that her attack on the tree hadn't had its desired effect. After all, the merlin was just trying to get by, like all of us were.

The radio stayed off the whole day. I guess the voice meant for people to spend this time with their loved ones, to say good-bye, although I never asked and Pete never said. Pete wasn't saying much of anything, but he did come down and sit with us for a while.

Mom joined us as well, so that at one point we were all together at the same table for the first time since Dad turned to glass. Mom raised her hands and pressed them together, then lowered her head, apparently deciding that someone should finally finish what Dad had started before our last meal.

"Thank you, Lord," she began, "for the wonderful years that you've given us, for the joy and memories and all the laughter. We've truly been blessed. Thank you for letting me be here for Peter and Ben, and for giving us all the strength we need to get through this. Thank you as well for accepting Dean into heaven, and for keeping him safe there. I know that you'll do the same for each of us when our time comes, so that one day we can all be together again in your light. Amen."

"Amen," Pete and I both said, although I had never actually lowered my head and put my hands together. I wasn't sure how I felt about giving thanks to a god who didn't seem capable of helping us, who had left us to deal with everything on our own.

We sat in silence for a while after Mom finished, and I watched as tears began to form in the corners of her eyes.

"Your dad thought the world of you boys," she said at length. "And your uncle Dean did as well. They were good men, both of them, and you will be, too. I guess in some ways you already are." She sighed, as if troubled by this realization that our childhoods were over, which they definitely were.

Pete and I didn't say anything, just glanced sideways at each other, both of us knowing what was to come, but not what would follow.

FORTY-EIGHT

The hands on the clock moved forward, while upstairs the voice droned on with what I assumed was probably an eleventh-hour call for resolve, and a reminder to all those who were listening that this might be our only shot, our one chance to shift the balance of power in our favor.

The message was far too muffled for me to make out from my place in the dining room, but it was easy enough to imagine the words. I could feel them, too, their vibration spreading out through the floor and the walls, like a billion termites intent on bringing the house down around me.

I sat at the table feeling strangely charged, as if I'd been soaking up pure electricity while I slept, in preparation for what was to come. I was surprised that I even *had* slept, but I guess sometimes the body just takes what it needs, regardless of whether or not the mind wants it.

I had a weapon in the form of a thick piece of kindling on the table before me, one that I'd picked from my pile of firewood during the night. I wouldn't use it unless I had to, but it was here for me if I did. I kept telling myself that Pete would back down once he saw how serious I was, once he realized just how far I was prepared to go in protecting Dad, but deep down I wasn't sure that he actually would.

Would there be a countdown? Would Pete have his stopwatch set to it?

Maybe I could stall him long enough for the shattering to happen without him. Maybe I could hold him back until the sky went quiet and began to clear, offering proof that the plan was working without him, without Dad. But that was assuming that the plan even *would* work. I wasn't sure about that either.

I couldn't sit still anymore. A surplus of nervous energy demanded that I get up and move. I walked over to the living room window and opened the curtains all the way, the dull gray light of the day washing over me.

A big brown jackrabbit was on our lawn, munching on the stems of dandelions that had gone to seed. It darted away when it saw me, but it didn't go far. It had been weeks since anyone had bothered to cut their grass, so there were dandelions everywhere.

Mom quietly came into the room and stood beside me, saying nothing.

I still wasn't sure where she planned to be when the time for the shattering finally arrived. Asleep in her bedroom, I hoped, or at least upstairs, perhaps lulled into some half-conscious state by a silver tongue and a sea of static. Whatever happened, I didn't want her to be right there to see it. I didn't want her to have to remember, to relive it whenever her mind slipped into the past. As mad as I was at her, and as betrayed as I felt, I couldn't help but worry about afterward.

Mom followed my gaze to where the jackrabbit had relocated.

"Oh," she said, "look at that."

I wasn't sure how to reply. All I could think of was a broken goshawk dying in a hole, its traitorous talons still grasping.

We stood there in silence for what seemed like forever, until finally Mom took a deep breath and let it out slow. "I know it's hard, Ben," she softly said to me. "It's the hardest thing ever. We're going to be okay, though. I promise."

She gave my arm a gentle but reassuring squeeze.

Not all of us, I thought. *Not if you and Pete and most of the world get your way.* I couldn't even bring myself to look at her.

She left the room as quietly as she had come in, but not before going over to kiss Dad on the forehead, which brought tears to my eyes, and made me wonder how love and betrayal could occupy the very same space at the very same moment, like two particles somehow defying the laws of the universe.

The clock on the wall kept ticking, the seconds and minutes turning into hours. One o'clock soon became two o'clock; two o'clock soon became three.

My hands were sweating, my heart pounding in anticipation.

Pete didn't come out of our room until just a few minutes to four. By then I had flipped the table over and turned it up on its side, rotating the entire thing so that Dad was behind it. I had moved the chair and the couch as well, ensuring that if Pete were to reach Dad, he would first have to get through me.

Pete came down the stairs carrying a hammer, the same black-and-green one that I'd watched Dad use to build a birdhouse for Mom last spring. The birdhouse was hanging up in the backyard, from a tree near the bushes along the fence. Mom's sparrows had claimed it almost immediately after it was put there.

Pete's eyes were so red he almost looked like a zombie. His body was tense, his mouth a grim line. He paused when he saw me standing there with my thick chunk of kindling.

"Get out of my way, Ben," he said, his voice profoundly tired yet resolute.

I looked at the clock again, saw that it was 3:58 p.m. on the nose. "You're early," I told him.

"I figured it would take me a couple of minutes to talk some sense into you," he replied.

"I'm not moving," I said, taking a step toward

him, my heart doing double-time in my chest, crashing against my rib cage like something trapped and trying to break out.

"Don't make me hurt you," he warned me. "I don't want to hurt you. I just want this to all be over. Aren't you tired, Ben? Haven't you had enough?" His fingers tightened on the grip of the hammer.

If someone had asked me a few minutes earlier, I would have said that I was positive Pete wouldn't hit me with something like that, something that could fracture a skull or break a bone clean in half, but I was beginning to have doubts. There was something in my brother's eyes that I didn't like. A glint that reminded me of Mom with the chain saw.

I felt a moment of genuine fear, but then something inside me shifted, displacing the fear with anger. My body went from being a vessel for anxious energy to something combustible, something that might explode if placed too close to a fire.

Pete glanced down at his watch and then up at me. "I don't have time for this, Ben," he said.

I just set myself square in his path.

"Fine," he said. "Have it your way." And then he

charged, faking left before going right. It was a move that I knew had fooled numerous goalies over the years, which was how I anticipated it.

I dropped into a crouch and surged forward, dropping my weapon as I tackled Pete around the waist. We both went crashing over the arm of the couch and onto the floor, where I managed to grab Pete's shirt and pull it over his head so that he couldn't see—another trick I'd learned from watching hockey.

He swore and let go of the hammer, freeing both of his hands up to wrestle me off him. I saw the hammer bounce off the living room carpet and then heard it clatter to a stop on the linoleum in the dining room.

I gasped as Pete slammed an elbow into my ribs, and then doubled over as he landed a solid punch to my stomach, but I didn't let go. His shirt was no longer over his eyes, but I still had it wrapped around one of my hands, preventing him from getting up from his knees to his feet.

"Let go!" he screamed, punching me again.

I grunted and pulled down harder, then rolled my hip so that we both flopped sideways. It had to be four o'clock now, I was sure.

I looked up in order to find out exactly where the second hand was, but what I saw instead was Mom, pushing the table aside to stand next to Dad, the green-and-black hammer now in her hand.

All the fight went out of me as I saw what was coming: the hammer arcing up as Mom lifted her arm. Pete felt my body go slack and turned his head then, too, so that both of us were looking at Dad, so that both of us saw the twin points of pure white light appear in his eyes.

The sparrows arrived at that very moment, banging against the back window with their feet and their wings.

"Wait!" Pete and I both yelled, our voices sounding as one.

Mom tried to check her swing, but the momentum was too strong to counter. She couldn't stop the motion completely, just slow it down. The hammer fell, struck glass, but gently, oh so gently.

There was the tiniest *plink* sound, and then nothing for the space of a second or two, long enough for a spark of hope to flash into being inside me.

The two spots of light began to grow, while outside the sparrows kept shrieking and whistling and chirping.

Songbirds they might have been, but this wasn't song; it wasn't anything anyone anywhere had ever heard from the beaks of birds. It was a message borne by a flock unequipped to deliver it, and yet somehow I understood. Somehow I knew that what they were saying was simply this: *He's with us. He's here.*

A tiny crack appeared at the point of impact, and began to lengthen, branching down like tree roots or lightning, like so many tributaries from a river as black as night.

I didn't know where to look, at the cracks now racing wildly across Dad's surface, or at the intensifying light that was spreading out from his eyes as well, following those very same fissures of potential destruction, and giving the impression of a jet-black statue weeping tears of pure white radiance.

Time slowed. For a moment it might have stopped altogether. I breathed, in and out, in and out, again and again as fate flipped a coin to make up its mind, and then all at once the world returned to real time. The cracks reached the tips of Dad's fingers and the ends of his toes, a thousand tiny fault lines with nowhere left to branch to.

The shattering was instantaneous. Dad was there and then he wasn't. The world skewed sideways. The birds fell silent.

I watched as the last few fragments rained down from the edge of the chair to the floor below. For a moment I was too stunned to move, but then I leaped up and ran to him, collapsing to my knees and grabbing up handfuls of the glass, the fragments so small and fine that they simply poured through my fingers like sand. The light, of course, was gone now.

Mom was weeping, Pete just standing there with his mouth open, disbelieving.

I stared at him, while above me the muffled sound of the radio through the floor abruptly stopped, its sudden absence a sharp reminder of what had brought us here to this moment.

Hatred filled me as I got to my feet, hatred and blame. Pete was no longer my brother or my enemy; he was simply a target for the guided missile of my rage, a target that must be destroyed. I leaped across the room toward him. I'm not sure my feet ever touched the ground. He could have stepped back or sideways, or simply raised his arms to block me, but he didn't.

He put up no resistance at all as we fell to the floor. Nor did he try to fight back when I closed my fists and began to throttle him, my jaw clenched so hard that my molars should have cracked.

"Go on, Ben," he told me as I pummeled him. "Go on."

But then I couldn't. His refusal to fight back just made it all sour, and as quickly as it had come, the hatred was gone.

Mom pulled me off him and tried to hold me, my knuckles bloody against her dress. I struggled free of her grasp, grief settling like a ten-pound rock in the pit of my stomach. I felt sick, feverish. I had to get out of there while I still could, before adrenaline left me spent and weeping upon the floor.

I ran.

Out the front door and down the street, tears building in my eyes, blurring everything. It didn't matter. The world wasn't worth seeing anyway. Not anymore.

FORTY-NINE

I didn't stop running until I reached the big maple tree in the corner of Sunskill Park, at which point I started climbing, the limbs so familiar to me that I didn't even have to think about where I was putting each hand or foot.

Pete and I had climbed this tree more times than I could remember, and unlike the one in our backyard, it required almost no effort at all. The first branches were low, and the middle ones spaced close together. The only real challenge it offered was in height. Pete sometimes dared to go almost three-quarters of the way to the top, whereas I always stopped just below that point, not trusting the limbs beyond to reliably hold my weight.

Today I would test them; today I would venture all the way up to where a checkered kite had been lodged for years, the fabric attached to its frame now tattered and torn by so many seasons of wind and rain and snow. Today I would free the kite—as Pete had tried to on many occasions—and not even think about the dangers in doing so...at least not until afterward, when the flex of the branches beneath me finally began to register in my grief- and anger-addled brain.

One of the branches actually broke off below me, but I managed to land on another as I fell, my hands sliding along the trunk, which was hardly even trunk-like this high up.

The close call sent a shiver of panic through me, and forced me to lower myself farther and find a thick branch to sit on while I waited for my hands to stop shaking and my nerves to settle. The sound of the sparrows outside our window wouldn't leave my mind, and neither would the sight of those bright white veins, branching out from Dad's unseeing eyes. It all kept repeating inside my brain, but not like a proper memory. It was hazy around the edges, like something I had dreamed or simply made up. Like an illusion some hypnotist planted there. In my heart, though, I knew it was true.

I'm not really sure when the sky started clearing. Somehow I didn't notice the change until it was complete, with unbroken blue stretching out as far as I could see in every direction. I had gotten so used to there not being color above me that it seemed strangely oversaturated now, almost to the point of not looking real. I could hardly believe that anything in the world could even *be* so blue. I sat there blinking in awe of it.

Pete appeared at the base of the tree shortly thereafter. He picked up the tattered kite and looked it over as if it were a relic from some bygone age, which in a way I guess it was. He set it back down and said to me, "I'm coming up."

He did, but he took his time, plotting his way with the same timid care that I always took. For a moment we had switched roles, with me being the kite-chasing daredevil and him the cautious follower. He settled into his usual spot, which today was just below me instead of just above.

I waited for him to say something, for him to tell me that the shattering had worked, but it would be hours and days yet before either of us really knew that for sure. Pete didn't say anything. He just sat there with me in silence, his lip all busted up and swollen, his left eye looking like mine had after the tea shop.

"It could have been different," I finally said to him.

He nodded without looking up at me. "Yeah," he said. "I guess."

The leaves on the maple were just beginning to turn, summer green giving way to autumn reds and yellows. Pete had a habit of picking leaves and tearing them along their veins, an absentminded dissection that resulted in a slow rain of forage for the many ants that lived in a colony at the base of the tree trunk. Pete never took notice of the ants (except when they crawled on him), but it didn't matter; the industrious insects benefitted from his destruction all the same.

He reached out now as I'd seen him reach out before, only this time he paused just short of a leaf, and then gently drew his hand back.

FIFTY

A whole month went by without incident, and then two. We finally began to allow ourselves to believe that it was over, that we could let go of our lingering dread and try to move on, however difficult that might be.

A new pastor arrived from out west to take over at church, his youthful energy and lively sermons a sharp contrast to Pastor Nolan's more solemn demeanor. The new organ player was young as well, and almost seemed to bounce as she fingered the keys. I tried not to think about all the empty spots on the pews, or the empty spots in the hearts of those who remained. Mrs. Crandall still came every Sunday, but just on her own, as Mr. Crandall was no better off now than when he first returned. The shattering might well have worked, but those who had come back before had clearly lost something that couldn't be returned, no matter how large the sacrifice.

School started up again just after Christmas. Lester Messam had a permanent limp now and seemed diminished in his brother's absence, and although there were times when both Pete and I caught him looking at us out on the playground or in the hallways, he hadn't yet tried to exact any sort of revenge. Maybe he was just biding his time, but after everything that had happened during the glass plague, it's possible he just lost his nerve. I wasn't really worried either way. I heard that Lester was living with his uncle now, and that he'd lost his father during the dark days, too, but not from the shattering. James Messam had apparently drank himself into the grave shortly after Lars disappeared and didn't come home again (on the day of the fire). I hoped that, for Lester's sake, his uncle was a better man than his dad had been.

A shortage of teachers meant that some of our classes had to be taught by volunteers. Mom decided she should be one of them. There were times when she still got anxious, and times when she still felt the need to take a step back, but for the most part she was getting through it. The guilt and sadness that I feared might cripple her was instead being channeled into a gift of pure generosity, which would have filled Dad's heart with gladness. I imagined him smiling at the sight of her standing there at the chalkboard, an eraser in one hand and a pointer in the other. The glass plague might have passed her over, but she was nevertheless transformed.

Holga returned in February, with a U-Haul trailer packed full of her belongings and multiple crates of tea, as well as a healthy supply of salty black licorice.

In early March, a huge flock of Bohemian waxwings visited our yard. For three days in a row, thousands of them came to feed in our mountain ash tree. They tossed the frozen berries into the air and swallowed them whole; they hung upside down and picked them like hungry acrobats; sometimes they fed them to each other, the berries passed gently from one bill to the next.

Mom and I watched from below, while Pete ran in

circles around us and tried his best to get a few good pictures. A photography project for art class had opened his mind to a whole new world.

Nobody talked about the shattering. Nobody celebrated the fact that it had worked. Life simply went on.

There was no mention anywhere of anyone changing like Dad did, with veins of pure white light branching out from the blackness. He would have been the first, I believed—a soul claimed by darkness and carried away by crows, and then rescued by a host of fearless sparrows.

I believed this, but I could never know for sure, could never prove it, so I had to let it go. I had to accept that the plan had worked, and that Pete had been right all along. I had to forgive him, just as I had to forgive Mom for taking his side, for not trusting in me. I had to forgive them because we were a family, and there's nothing more important than family.

Our sparrows resumed being sparrows and never left us again, all except for one female with decidedly angelic wings. I hadn't seen the leucistic bird since the day that we lost Dad for good, and while it's perfectly reasonable to think that a predator might have gotten her—either our merlin or a visiting sharp-shinned hawk—somehow I just didn't buy that. I'd always thought of the white-winged anomaly as being Mom's special bird, but maybe it was Dad that she was here for all along. I like to imagine she's with him still, and that maybe she helped him to get where he needed to go.

And as for the voice on the radio, he never did reveal who he was or where he was broadcasting from. The station simply went silent after the shattering, or rather it returned to static, which, as Dad had once explained to us, was actually the sound of the universe, the white-noise echo of all the energy released at the moment of the big bang, at the very instant of our creation. A voice from the beginning of time, I guess you could say.

ACKNOWLEDGMENTS

I think sometimes in life we need to take a step back in order to move forward. Such was the case with this book. After an inspired start, I soon lost my momentum, and then my faith in myself and in my future as a writer. So I took a step back, and threw myself into learning about and photographing birds. I could never have known it at the time, but this new passion would ultimately fuel my old one and provide me with just the synergy I needed to bring a stagnating work-in-progress back to life. I think birds are amazing creatures and that we should all be inspired by them.

Thank you to my awesome agent, Ali Herring, for your wisdom, your kindness, and all your hard work. I'm forever grateful. Thank you to Michael Strother, Deirdre Jones, and the entire team at LBYR for turning this dream into a reality. Your enthusiasm and your vision in developing this project have meant the world to me.

Thank you to all the short-fiction editors who have published me over the years. Like a lot of writers, I cut my teeth on the short stuff before ever tackling a novel, and I feel that this has been integral to my growth as a storyteller. This particular novel was actually built upon the bones of one of my short stories.

Thank you to all my friends for your continued positivity and support, especially Ross Kimble, for the early encouragement and help. Thank you to my family for cheering me on and for believing that I had this in me. Thanks especially to my mom, whose tearful reaction to my very first short story told me I was on the right path, and also to my siblings, without whom I would not have had the experience to draw from in capturing the essence of Ben and Pete's relationship.

Most of all, thank you to Anna, for being my rock and the love of my life since we were just a couple of kids way back in high school. By turns you have been my best friend, my beta reader, my sounding board, and the person who has picked me up whenever I've fallen. You've seen me at my best and at my worst, and yet somehow your faith in me has never wavered. I could never have gotten here without you.